# DÉJÀ VU DREAMS

## MARSHA DEFILIPPO

To get the latest information on new releases, excerpts and more, be sure to sign up for Marsha's newsletter.

https://marshadefilippo.com/newsletter

ALSO BY MARSHA DEFILIPPO

Arizona Dreams

Coming April 2022

*Disillusioned Dreams*

To get the latest information on new releases, excerpts and more, be sure to sign up for Marsha's newsletter.

https://marshadefilippo.com/newsletter

CHAPTER ONE

*What the hell was I thinking?!*

The blast of arctic air that assaulted Sharon Peterson as she stepped outside the terminal at Bangor International Airport was in stark contrast to the 79 degrees at the airport in Tucson when she'd started her trip earlier that day. She looked to her left and saw the taxi she'd arranged to have pick her up and headed in that direction.

"Hi, I texted earlier," she said to the driver.

"Right. You're Sharon Peterson?" he asked.

"That's right," she replied.

"Hop in and we'll get you home," he said as he took her carryon bag from her and put it in the cab's trunk.

Sharon was returning from her first winter as a snowbird. She'd originally planned to be there with her husband, Tom, but he had passed away after a bout with an aggressive form of cancer shortly before they were scheduled to leave. It had been a much different winter for other reasons as well. She'd expected it to be lonely, but on a whim she'd signed up for a class to decorate gourds and had met Donna Mackenzie, who had turned out to be a good friend. Joseph Ramos, the contractor who had built the home she and Tom were to share, had also become a good friend. Most unexpected, though, was her budding romance with Hal Jackson. She'd met him on an unplanned trip to Sedona. He was also a snowbird with a winter home in Tucson and was a retired graphic designer. Never in her life would she have thought she would become romantically involved after losing Tom. Life hands you many surprises.

It was a quick ride back to her home just outside Bangor and she was glad she'd had Gary Smith from A-1 Handyman Services looking after it while she was away. Gary had turned up the heat and left a light on for her, knowing she'd be arriving late at night, so she wasn't coming home to a dark house. She took her carryon bag into her bedroom after hanging her coat in the closet and then walked through the house, not so much to make sure no one was there who shouldn't be, but to familiarize herself with this house again. After living there for over 25 years, it did seem odd to her she would need to do that but being away for over three months made it seem like she was a stranger in her own house. It wasn't something she had imagined could happen, but perhaps it was that so many other things had changed her life as well that she needed to establish herself here again.

She'd hoped taking the later flight out of Tucson and arriving at nearly 11 PM in Maine would help with the jet lag, but she found she was still wired, and it would probably be a while before sleep overtook her.

*Maybe a cup of chamomile tea will help,* she told herself.

She put the teakettle on to boil the water, got herself a cup, and found the packet of tea in the cupboard. She leaned up against the counter as her mind drifted while she waited for the water to boil. Her next day's to do list went through her mind, with the first on the list being inviting her daughters to come for dinner the next evening. She wasn't sure why she hadn't told them before this that she was dating someone and that it might be serious. Serious enough that they had made plans for him to come to Maine to visit her to keep the relationship going while they were on their non-snowbird schedules. She expected Jessica to be okay with the news, but it was more likely that Amanda would be upset. Mandy and Tom had been very close, even though he was not her biological father. Sharon had divorced him when both girls were very young and had met and married Tom soon after the divorce. He had always been like their father and had even adopted them after he and Sharon married. Their biological father had never wanted to or been a part of their lives, so Tom was really the only father figure they had ever known. The tea kettle's whistle brought Sharon out of her reverie and, after putting a teaspoon of honey in the cup, she took it over to the couch and pulled up a blanket to take off the chill. Her body had acclimated to the warmer temperatures in Arizona and she'd felt the cold air even more than she otherwise would have had she spent the winter in Maine. The tea's warmth felt good on her hands and she held her face over the steam that rose from the cup to warm her face. Sipping that first taste calmed her as she felt the warmth go all the way down. Sighing contentedly, she turned her thoughts back to what she would need to do the next day.

First, call the girls and invite them to dinner.

Next, a trip to the grocery store to stock her cupboards again.

*Third?*

She found she was actually more tired than she had thought she would be now that she'd had a chance to relax. The trip had been uneventful but still, it had taken its toll on her body and between the trip, the tea, and finally being able to relax in her own home again, she realized she might be able to sleep much earlier than she'd thought.

*Take advantage of it now and get to bed,* she told herself. *You're going to need your strength tomorrow.*

# CHAPTER TWO

"Hi, Mom. Welcome home!" Jessica said as soon as she'd picked up the call.

"I'd say it's good to be here, and it is," Sharon added, "but I think next year I might wait until at least the middle of April and maybe the first of May before I come home," chuckling as she said it.

"What? You aren't enjoying this balmy day?" Jessica teased.

"Um, no, if I'm going to be honest about it," Sharon replied. "I think waking up to 30 degrees after being used to 60s wasn't something I'd prepared for. Live and learn, though. What I'd really called for, besides hearing your voice again, was to invite you and Mandy to come over for dinner tonight to catch up. Do you have plans or could you come?"

"No plans, and I'd love to see you. I've missed you!" Jessica answered.

"I've missed you, too, sweetie," Sharon told her. "Just come over when you get off work and we can eat around 6:30. Does that work for you?"

"Perfect! I can't wait to see you. Is there anything I can bring?"

"Just yourself," Sharon answered. "I have to do a grocery run today anyway, so I'll get anything I need then. Have a great rest of the day and I'll see you soon. Love you!"

"Love you, too, Mom. See you later."

Sharon realized she was tensing as she clicked off and brought up her Favorites contact list to call Mandy.

*No need to get stressed out yet*, she told herself. *And maybe you're just projecting anyway*, she tried to reassure herself.

She clicked the phone and heard the line ringing as she took a deep breath in and out to settle herself.

"Mom! Welcome back! How was your flight?" Mandy asked.

"Luckily, an uneventful one. Those are the best kind," Sharon smiled upon hearing Mandy's voice. "I could have used some warmer temps, but you can't have everything. I just told Jess that I will probably stay a little longer next winter to avoid that."

"At least it wasn't snowing!" Mandy laughed.

"So true. Be grateful for small blessings, I guess. I was calling to invite you to come for dinner tonight so we can catch up. I was thinking dinner around 6:30 but come earlier if you're able to get out of work on time."

"That would be great!" Mandy replied. "Can I bring anything?"

"No, that's okay. Just yourself will be all I need."

"See you tonight. Love you, Mom!"

"Love you, too!" Sharon replied.

She exhaled a deep breath, but realizing that was the easy part, she would need to take some time before they arrived to organize her thoughts about how to explain she was dating. It wasn't something she'd ever had to do since the kids were so young when she'd started dating Tom, or at least not in the same way that this would be. They'd liked Tom from the very first time she'd introduced him. Should this be a red flag that she was so nervous about telling them about Hal, or just normal nervousness since they were all at a different point in their lives? She hoped it was the latter.

Now that she'd gotten that out of the way, though, it was time to start her day in earnest with the grocery shopping first on the list.

# CHAPTER THREE

By that afternoon, she felt more settled and the feeling of being a stranger in her own home had mostly passed. She'd texted both Hal and Donna to let them know she'd made it back safely. She'd also let Hal know that she had plans for dinner with the girls so wouldn't be able to call until later after they'd gone, but with the time difference, it wouldn't be that late for him.

She had dinner prepped and ready to pop in the oven so that she could chat with the girls after they arrived.

She heard a knock just before the door opened and Jessica walked in.

"Look who I found prowling in your front dooryard," she announced, as Mandy came in right behind her.

"Oh, it's so great to see you both. Group hug!" Sharon declared as she walked to them and they encircled each other.

They broke the embrace, and the girls put their coats away before joining Sharon at the kitchen island seating area.

"What can I get you to drink? I have a fresh pot of coffee but there's also water, tea, a glass of wine?" Sharon asked.

"Coffee for me," Mandy answered.

"Just water for me," Jessica replied.

"Here you go." Sharon put the drinks in front of them and poured herself a cup of coffee.

"I know we've talked, but what haven't you told us yet?" Mandy asked.

Sharon hesitated as she was taken aback by the question.

"Mom?" Jess asked. "What's the matter? You look like you've seen a ghost."

"No, no, I guess I was just surprised as there is something I need to tell you both and have been dreading it a bit. I probably should have told you sooner and can't quite put my finger on why I didn't. It's nothing bad…," she added hastily upon seeing their expressions.

"I met someone, and we've been dating for the past month," she blurted.

This was not going according to plan, she realized, and needed to regroup to the script she'd run through her mind most of the day.

"What do you mean you've been dating?" Mandy asked in a tone that warned this could be going into dangerous territory.

"It all happened quite suddenly and very unexpectedly," Sharon answered, looking at both girls' faces. Jessica's was her usual calm self, not revealing what might be going on in her head, but Mandy's was clearly upset, as she'd feared it might be.

"I'd taken an unplanned trip to Sedona. I think I mentioned that before. When I was there, I met Hal. Hal Jackson is his full name. He was staying at the same motel and we met in the breakfast room. We struck up a conversation and then went hiking and ended up spending the next couple of days getting to know each other. He lives in Tucson during the winter and is divorced, a retired graphic designer, and a really nice guy," she added, realizing she was edging on babbling. This was definitely not going according to script.

She went on, as there was no response from either daughter.

"We realized we really enjoyed each other's company and continued to see each other once we got back from Sedona. We've made plans for him to come here to visit as we would like to continue the relationship, or at least explore whether we can make it work with a long-distance relationship. He's going to be coming here next week, so I wanted to let you know that was happening and I hope you'll like him and can be happy for me," she finished.

"Wow," was all Jessica managed.

Mandy's face said all Sharon needed to know. This was not going to be easy, just as she'd expected.

"How could you?" she finally blurted out. "Dad hasn't even been dead six months and you're already moving on?"

"Mandy, I know this must be hard for you. It wasn't anything I planned. It just happened," Sharon replied. "I still love your dad and I would never dishonor his memory, but I really don't think he would expect me to live the rest of my life alone. We talked about this before he died, but I never thought anything would actually happen, so dismissed it as not being anything to think twice about."

"Obviously," Mandy replied angrily. "I can't stay. This is just too much for me," she said as she got up and took her coat from the closet and left.

"Well, at least she didn't slam the door," Sharon tried to joke.

"Mom, I'm really confused right now, so please don't make light of this. It's a big deal," Jessica answered.

"I'm sorry, I'm trying to defuse the situation and that's not really fair," Sharon replied. "This really isn't how I was hoping to tell you girls."

"I guess that's not really true, if I'm going to be honest with myself," she went on. "I knew Mandy would be upset but was hoping she'd understand that I don't mean any disrespect to your father, and it wasn't as though I went out there hoping to hook up."

"*Mom!*" Jessica's face was shocked.

Sharon had to laugh despite herself. "I'm sorry, but you really should see your face."

Jessica hesitated and then laughed. "I guess it must be caption-worthy. I'm going to have to give myself some time to process all this."

"I understand. I've had over a month to process it, and I'm still not sure I have," Sharon replied. "Will you still stay for dinner, though? I've really missed you and don't want to end the evening being upset with each other."

"Sure, Mom," she said, and got up from her seat to give Sharon a hug.

The rest of the evening went much better, but the topic of Hal was left simmering on the back burner as they kept their conversations to anything but that.

"I'll give Mandy a call tomorrow and see if we can patch things up," Sharon told Jessica as she was leaving. "Hopefully she just needs a little time to let this sink in."

"Hopefully," Jess echoed. "Although knowing her, it may take more than a little time."

They hugged again, and Sharon closed the door after one last wave goodbye. She headed back to her bedroom, not quite as excited about calling Hal as she'd been earlier in the day, knowing he'd be asking how it went and not wanting to tell him there were storm clouds on the horizon.

CHAPTER FOUR

"Hello, Gorgeous."

"Hello, Handsome," Sharon replied with a smile on her face.

"How's it feel to be home?" Hal asked.

"Actually, a bit weird. I never imagined that I'd feel like my real home is Arizona and I'm just visiting here in Maine, but that's exactly how it feels. I'm sure that will pass as time goes on and I get acclimated to being back."

"That's probably true. I get a bit of that myself when I go back to Minnesota."

"Are you back in Tucson now?"

"Yeah, I got back sooner than I thought. Things went smoothly, so I was able to book a flight back this morning," Hal replied.

Although he was retired, Hal still did freelance work and had several regular clients with whom he did business. He had been out of town for a client meeting when Sharon had returned to Maine.

"That's good to hear it all went well," Sharon said.

"So, what have you been up to since you got back?"

"Grocery shopping and dinner with the girls were the high points. Although I'm not sure dinner was exactly a high point."

"Oh, what happened?" Hall asked.

Sharon sighed.

"It was going fine until I told the girls about us. To say Mandy was not pleased would be a major understatement. I'm not completely surprised but wasn't expecting the degree of pushback that I got."

"I suppose that's normal. It hasn't been that long since Tom died, and I take it they must have been close."

"Yes, they were very close. Not that Tom and Jessica weren't as well, but there was something special between him and Mandy from the very start. It's almost as though she was his biological daughter, they were so much alike."

"That puts an extra spin on it, for sure," Hal agreed. "Hopefully once she meets me, she'll be reassured that I only want to make you happy."

"That's what I'm hoping, too. I plan to invite her to come over for dinner tomorrow night so that we can talk about it. She left in a hurry last night and maybe with just the two of us and not having Jess here will help her feel more like she can speak her mind."

"I hope so, too. I can tell how it's upset you and I feel bad that I'm not there to give you a hug. I miss you, Sharon," Hal said.

"I miss you, too, Hal," Sharon replied.

They chatted for a few more minutes and then called it a night with a promise from Sharon that she would call the next night to let Hal know how it went.

# CHAPTER FIVE

The night was a restless one for Sharon and she woke up feeling drained. She'd spent most of it going over scenarios in her mind, knowing full well that there was no point in letting the "what ifs" rule her thinking. It was still too early to call, but after a light breakfast and shower, she texted Mandy with an invitation to come over that evening so they could talk.

It was a few tense moments of watching the phone screen before the dots appeared to indicate Mandy was typing a reply.

**I can be there by 6 if that works.**

Sharon breathed a sigh of relief and immediately texted back.

**That's perfect. See you then. Love you, Mom.**

**Love you, too. See you later.**

With that settled, Sharon was able to get through the rest of the day in a much better frame of mind, although still anxious about their discussion and, hopefully, resolution.

Promptly at 6, Sharon heard Mandy's car pull into the driveway and headed toward the door. She couldn't tell from Mandy's expression whether she was still in a mood but pulled her into her arms and gave her a big hug.

"Thank you for coming. I felt terrible about how we left

things last night." Sharon said as she hung Mandy's coat in the closet, and they walked into the living room and sat together on the couch.

"Me, too. I couldn't sleep most of the night and if you hadn't texted me first, I was going to text you first thing this morning. I wasn't sure how late you might sleep with the jet lag so didn't want to wake you."

"Jet lag wasn't my reason for not sleeping last night. I have a feeling we were both going through what we said. I'm hoping tonight will be different. I really don't want there to be this distance between us especially now that I've just gotten back and can be with you physically," Sharon went on.

"I'm sorry, Mom. I know I probably overreacted, but I'm still so sad about Dad dying and it was just too soon," Mandy said with tears welling in her eyes.

Sharon hugged her again and they sat there for a minute, with tears running down both their cheeks.

"I get it, honey. I really do," Sharon said as she wiped her tears and nose and handed Mandy a tissue. "Your Dad and I talked about this before he died, but I never brought it up with you girls because I never in a million years thought I would ever have the need to. Getting involved with someone, especially this soon, wasn't even on my radar when I got to Arizona. And the last thing I would ever want to do is to hurt you or Jess."

"Knowing Dad, I can imagine him telling you he wouldn't want you to be alone and unhappy, so I guess I should be okay with it. But why does it feel like you're being disloyal to his memory?" she looked at Sharon beseechingly.

"It feels a little like that to me, too. I would be lying if I said I don't have twinges of guilt because I do but then I remind myself of the kind of man that your dad was and that I truly can't imagine that he would want me to be sad and not moving on with my life. I don't know how this is going to turn out with Hal. It might be a rebound romance for all I know, but I'd like to give it the chance so I can find out and I hope you can be happy for me."

"I'll try, but it may take me a while," Mandy replied.

"That's fair. I had the benefit of those talks with your dad and we had come to an understanding, even though I felt like I was just humoring him. Like I said, the last thing I wanted to think about then was getting involved romantically again."

"That makes sense. It felt to me like you had jumped into this and pushed his memory aside like last week's news," Mandy agreed.

"No, no, that wasn't it at all. It was just... one of those things," Sharon said, shrugging her shoulders. "I know it sounds like a Lifetime Channel movie, but I guess sometimes these things really do happen."

Mandy smiled. "Well, let's hope it's not one of those ones that the widow gets taken by a con man before finding true love with the detective investigating the case."

"Yikes!" Sharon laughed. "I don't get the impression that's what's happening and although your dad left me well taken care of, it's not like anyone would be set for life taking my money. Hal seems to be doing quite well from his own money, but I admit we didn't trade balance sheets."

She hoped the joke was just that, but it put a bit of doubt in her mind that probably had more to do with her own insecurities about why Hal would want to be with her than about his being a con man.

"On that note, unless there's anything else you'd like to ask me, I hope we can put this behind us for now and you'll be okay with meeting Hal when he gets here next week."

Sharon could see the surprise on Mandy's face and her conflicting emotions, but in the end she said, "Sure, Mom. I'll do my best to reserve judgment until I've at least had the chance to meet him."

"That's all I can ask," Sharon smiled.

"But I can't promise I'm going to like him," Mandy pretended to pout as she crossed her arms over her chest.

They both laughed, and the mood felt lighter.

"Okay, okay. I get it." Sharon put her hands up in mock defeat. "But now, how about we have dinner and talk about less emotionally charged topics and you catch me up on all the things we didn't talk about while I was gone."

They spent the rest of the evening chatting amiably and after Mandy left, Sharon was able to go to bed with a lighter heart. That night's sleep was much more restful.

# CHAPTER SIX

The next week went by quickly for Sharon. She caught up with friends and family she hadn't been in touch with since she'd been out West and settled back into a routine. The sensation of being a stranger passed after just a couple days and other than her calls with Hal and Donna, Arizona was beginning to feel like her second home again.

The day finally came for Hal's arrival and Sharon gave her house a once-through again before heading to the airport. She'd bought new bedding for her bedroom, although had stopped short of buying a new mattress after numerous internal discussions about doing so. Perhaps she hadn't gotten over the feeling of being disloyal to Tom's memory as much as she'd thought. It had been easier in Arizona since they had never lived together in that house, but this was the one they'd shared for 25 years and the feeling of bringing an interloper into their house was in the back of her mind as much as she tried to dismiss it.

It was still brisk, although par for the course as far as Maine's April weather pattern was concerned, so she had bundled up and had the heat on in the car as she nervously watched the terminal doors. Hal had texted as soon as the plane landed and let her know he only had a carryon so wouldn't need to wait for his luggage at Baggage Claim. Sharon had opted to wait at the curb rather than using the parking garage as it rarely took that long and traffic was usually light, especially at that time of night in Bangor. The expression, they roll up the side-walks at 9 wasn't just an old saying here.

Her heartbeat quickened as she saw him coming out of the terminal. and opened her door to get out and wave so he would see where she was parked. He smiled that George Clooney smile, and she melted, feeling silly even as it happened. She pressed the button to release the hatchback and then walked toward him to give him a hug. He pulled her into his embrace and kissed her.

"I've missed you," he whispered as they broke the kiss.

"I've missed you, too," she whispered back.

A blast of wind took them both by surprise, and Sharon shivered.

"Whoa, you weren't kidding about the temperatures. You'd think I'd be used to it after living in Minnesota all those years. I guess I've been spoiled living in Tucson."

"I've got the heat on in the car, so you won't have to be cold for long. Just toss your suitcase in the back and we can get on our way," Sharon replied.

"How was the flight?" she asked as she pulled out of the parking spot and headed toward home.

"Long, but no problems with connections, so I guess that makes it a good flight," he answered, echoing the words she'd used just the week before. "How long does it take to get to your house?"

"Only about 15 to 20 minutes and this time of night that should be on the shorter end of things."

They chatted about banal topics along the way and as promised, in 15 minutes they pulled into Sharon's driveway, and she parked inside the two-car attached garage.

"Nice house, just what I'd pictured for New England," Hal commented.

Sharon's house was a two-story colonial style, white with green shutters and a three-season porch on one end.

"Let's get inside and I'll give you the tour."

They walked into a mudroom that led into the open-concept kitchen/great room area. From there, Sharon led him into the formal dining room along the back of the house adjacent to the kitchen. The double French doorway at the end of the dining room led to the three-season porch.

A small hallway ran to the front foyer of the house with a door on the right leading to the basement. Stairs went up to the second floor on the right and a half bath on the left. They stopped to hang their coats in the closet between the stairs and hallway. Straight ahead was a formal living room with a fireplace and another set of double French doors also connecting to the three-season porch. Upstairs were two bedrooms on the left and a full bathroom directly ahead of the stairway and on the opposite side a third bedroom to the left and the Master Bedroom en suite to the right.

"Very nice," Hal said. "It was definitely a family home. I like where we ended up."

He put his suitcase down and took Sharon in his arms.

"I've been wanting to do this from the minute I saw you," he murmured, taking her in his arms and kissing her slowly and deeply.

Sharon returned his kiss, feeling her knees weaken.

"I've missed you and this," she said as they broke the embrace.

"I'm here now. I don't want to waste a minute of the time we have together," he said before kissing her again on the lips and then moving to her neck in that spot that always made her knees weak. He unbuttoned her blouse and kissed her in the bare spot above her bra, cupping her other breast in his left hand. With his right, he undid her bra and then removed both her shirt and bra.

Sharon stroked his back and let him lead the way for a moment before unbuttoning his shirt and stroking his chest, pressing hers against his, feeling the softness of his chest hair against her skin.

Hal walked her to the bed and pushed her gently onto her back before unbuttoning and unzipping her jeans and pulling them, along with her undies, down at the same time.

"Let me….. "

"Shhhhh," he interrupted. "I'm in charge…. for now," he said as he removed her shoes and socks.

He continued to kiss her, starting again at her lips and moving his way down her body as she moaned softly.

"Hal, please, I want to feel you next to me without your clothes."

He sat up and removed his shirt as she unbuttoned his jeans. He stood up to take them down the rest of the way along with his shoes and socks and then laying down next to her.

Their lovemaking was slow, as if they each wanted to savor every minute of their reunion until, at last, they both reached their climax.

"That was wonderful," Sharon whispered as they snuggled together under the covers afterwards.

"You're wonderful," Hal replied.

They drifted off to sleep, Sharon spooned next to Hal and his arm wrapped over her body.

She awoke the next morning and slipped out from under his arm to go downstairs. She didn't want to wake him but heard him speak as she was opening the bedroom door.

"Good morning. Where are you off to?"

"I'm sorry. I hope I didn't wake you," she replied and returned to the bed to give him a kiss. "I'm going downstairs to make some coffee. Would you like to sleep some more or are you ready to start your day?"

"I'm ready. I don't want to waste a minute with you," he smiled up at her. "What's on the agenda for today?"

"Well, I thought we could spend the first few days on our own showing you around. It's not going to be as nice as it would be in the summer, but the upside is that there will be fewer tourists."

"Sounds like a plan. What's on the agenda for the end of the week?"

"I was thinking we could have Jess and Mandy over for dinner so you could meet."

"That's a good idea. I'm hoping to win Mandy over and it sounds like Jess has kept an open mind from what you've said."

"Let's hope so," she smiled somewhat hesitantly.

"Still worried, though?"

"A bit, but no point bringing negative energy into the mix. Have to think positively, right?"

"Good attitude," he answered, smiling.

"You're welcome to use the shower now while I get the coffee ready, and it should be done by the time you are. Would you like some breakfast, too? I have all the fixings."

"I didn't realize I was hungry, but just the mention of it, has made my stomach growl. Eggs and bacon, maybe some toast?"

"Coming right up," she said and kissed him once more before heading down to the kitchen.

After finishing their breakfast and Sharon's turn in the shower, they headed out for the day, which had started with bright sunshine and blue sky and a forecast for unseasonably warm temperatures.

"You must have brought the wonderful weather with you," Sharon teased.

"I live to serve," he teased back. "Where are we headed?"

"Since it's such a beautiful day, I thought we should take advantage of it and head to the coast. Acadia National Park is beautiful and then we can take a tour of Bar Harbor. There might not be much open there this time of year. It used to be that shops closed right after Labor Day and didn't open back up until Memorial Day. That's changed a little, although more so on the autumn end of the tourist season because of the leaf peepers. There isn't nearly as much traffic in the spring, so we may not find much to do. It's still pretty at the harbor, though. Maybe you'd like some lobster ice cream?"

"Lobster ice cream?" he asked incredulously.

Sharon laughed. "I know it sounds like a horrible combination, but it's not that bad. Not my favorite flavor, but worth trying."

"I think I'll reserve judgement on that."

The drive to Acadia was uneventful, and as Sharon had anticipated, the traffic was light. They stopped at the Visitor Center at Acadia and picked up a map before heading onto the trail that looped around the park.

"I didn't think to check the tide chart, so it may not be the right time of day to get the most out of Thunder Hole, but it's still worth a stop.

"Thunder Hole?" Hal asked.

"That's because of the noise the ocean makes when it crashes against the rocks. It's loudest at certain times of the day according to the tides, but as many times as I've been there, I always have to look up when that is. I think it's about an hour before high tide, but don't hold me to that. Like I said, though, unless we've hit it by accident, it won't make much difference other than to have a look around. If there's anything in particular that you want to look at while we're driving, let me know and I'll pull over if it's safe to do so."

"It is beautiful here," Hal commented. "I've always heard about the rocky Maine coast, but this is my first time visiting."

"To be honest, I like Schoodic Point even better. It's also part of Acadia National Park but to get there by car, you have to drive in the opposite direction, so it's not directly connected by land. I'm not sure if we'd have time to go there today, but it could be something we do another day."

"I'm leaving it all in your capable hands," Hal smiled at her.

They continued driving through the park, stopping at various scenic vistas along the way before heading up the drive to the summit of Cadillac Mountain. Sharon parked in the lot so they could get out to hike the trail overlooking the Atlantic Ocean.

"You'll probably want your jacket," Sharon advised. "It can be windy and it's still only April even though today is warmer than normal."

Hal got his jacket from the back seat and joined her on the trail.

The scene from there was picture postcard perfect. Not a cloud in the sky and the sun warmed them. The view was amazing as it took in the Atlantic, which was relatively calm that day, and they could see boats bobbing up and down in the ocean. They walked along the trail to go out farther, holding hands, a slight breeze ruffling their hair.

"I can see why you want to stay here most of the year," Hal told her. "It's beautiful."

"It is," Sharon agreed. "I could never leave Maine even as much as I love Arizona, too. They've both become home to me now, but this is where my roots are. My family goes back to some of the first settlers in Maine and I have lines back to the Mayflower."

"Have you done much genealogy research into your ancestors?" Hal asked.

"Not really but have read some of the reports other relatives have done," Sharon replied. "I do like hearing about the connections but haven't ever been motivated to take it the next step to do my own searches. How about you? Do you know much about your family history?"

"No, it's not really something I've been interested in either. I know we've been here three or four generations, but that's as much as I know."

They enjoyed the view a few more minutes before deciding to head back to the car and onto the rest of the Park's drives.

"If you're getting hungry, we can see if the restaurant at Jordan Pond is open to grab some lunch. They're known for their popovers. It's a little pricey by Maine standards, but the food is usually good, and it shouldn't be a problem getting in," Sharon suggested.

"I am getting a little hungry. Must be the fresh air."

They lucked out and were able to stop for lunch, including the famous popovers.

"Don't forget to save room for the lobster ice cream," Sharon teased.

Hal groaned before replying, "I suppose I should just for the novelty of saying I've had it. Do they serve it here?"

"Not here," Sharon replied. "We'll need to head into Bar Harbor. There's a little ice cream shop there where we can find it. We can walk around a bit there first to get your appetite going again if you're too full now."

"I'd like the walk with or without the ice cream, but I did say I'd at least try it."

"You do know I'm not going to force you to finish it if you don't like it, right? You don't have to be a hero and eat it anyway. I'm not going to be offended," Sharon reassured him.

"No, of course not. Well, maybe I was a little worried I might offend you since you seem to be making a point of it."

Sharon wasn't completely sure if Hal was genuinely upset or not but decided to let it go. She didn't want to ruin their day by getting into an argument.

"If you're all set, we can get the check settled and be on our way," was all she chose to say.

They finished their tour of Acadia and headed toward Bar

Harbor. As she'd expected, there was very little traffic this time of year and they easily found a parking spot close enough to the town's center that they wouldn't have far to walk. The harbor was quiet although there were some boats tied up at the dock and they were able to spend time looking out at the expanse of ocean glinting in the sun; the air filled with the smell of the ocean and the sounds of the gulls squawking as they flew overhead, looking for handouts. They looked through the shops that were open, mostly catering to the tourist crowd's penchant for t-shirts and novelty items, but some also had a nice inventory of handmade crafts and artwork. Before heading back to the car and the drive back to Sharon's house, they found the ice cream shop featuring the lobster ice cream and bought just one dish to share.

"I hate to admit it, but you were right. This is actually pretty good," Hal told her somewhat begrudgingly.

"I'll refrain from saying I told you so," Sharon teased.

"I think you just did," Hal joked in reply. "Maybe we need to buy another one for the road."

Sharon raised her eyebrow in response but said nothing while Hal got out of the car and bought another serving.

"Good to go?" she asked as he got back in the car.

"Yup," he replied sheepishly as he scooped out a big spoonful and popped it in his mouth.

She just smiled and pulled the car out onto the street, heading back to Bangor. They returned home close to dinnertime, tired but happy from their first day together in Maine.

## CHAPTER SEVEN

They spent the next few days traveling to visit scenic spots in the area on day trips. The weather was unusually cooperative for April and the sunny, warm temperatures held. The mood was fun, and the romance continued.

"I'd like to invite Jess and Mandy to meet you on Saturday and was thinking it might be better to go to a restaurant to be on neutral ground," Sharon told Hal during breakfast on Thursday.

"That works for me. I'm looking forward to meeting them," Hal replied.

"I admit I was being a bit selfish and wanted to spend time just with you, but I don't want the time to slip by and I really do need to make sure they don't have something on their schedules."

"Absolutely. Why don't you give them a call or text now while I go take my shower?" he suggested.

"Great idea!"

Jessica promptly answered Sharon's text with a positive reply, followed shortly after by Mandy's agreement. They picked a time and restaurant that worked for all of them, and Sharon breathed easier. She knew she'd been putting off making the arrangements, not entirely because she wanted to spend more time with Hal. Even though she and Mandy had talked, she wasn't convinced that the introduction would go smoothly. Maybe she had been rushing things, but life doesn't always go according to plans. As the expression goes, somewhat para-phrased, people make plans and God laughs.

On Saturday, they met at the appointed time. Jessica had arrived first and was at the table waiting for them.

"Is Mandy here?" Sharon asked Jess.

"She had to use the Ladies Room but should be out soon," Jess replied.

"Jess, I'd like you to meet Hal Jackson. Hal, my daughter Jessica," Sharon introduced them.

"Really nice to meet you," Hal said as he extended his hand to shake hers. "Your mom has told me a bit about you. All good, of course," he smiled that charming smile.

Sharon was focused on Jess's face for her reaction and real-ized she'd been holding her breath. She couldn't read anything amiss with Jess's expression, so hoped that at least on that count, the evening would go smoothly. That optimism disappeared as she looked up to see Mandy approaching their table. Clearly, the expression on her face did not bode well. Although not exactly angry, her expression was closed and not welcoming. The promise to be open-minded may have disappeared since their conversation.

Sharon gave Mandy a hug when she got to their table and whispered in her ear, "Please be nice."

Mandy hugged her back and whispered, "I'll try."

They broke their embrace, and Sharon made the introduction with Hal.

"Your mom let me know that you might have some problems with my being here," Hal started. "I can completely understand that, but I hope you'll give me a chance to prove my intentions with her are honorable."

Mandy shook his hand and smiled, although it was forced.

"I do hope so," she replied. "My mom deserves that and that's how my dad always treated her," she added, the point being plain to everyone.

"Well, let's all sit down and get to know each other," Sharon interjected, hoping to move things along and switch topics.

The server arrived to take their drink orders and give them a few minutes to decide on their dinner choices.

"So, have you been enjoying your visit so far?" Jessica asked.

"I have," Hal replied enthusiastically. "Your mom is a great tour guide and Maine is a beautiful state."

"April isn't the best month to visit, but it can still be a pretty time of year," Jess said.

"If you like rain and mud and naked trees," Mandy responded.

Everyone laughed.

"When do your trees get leaves? I was wondering about that but hadn't asked."

"It varies, but this far north, it can be early to mid-May before they really bud out," Sharon answered. "You'll need to come back again so you can see the state when it's even prettier."

"When do you plan to come back again?" Mandy asked, although she didn't appear to want that to happen, judging by her body language.

"We hadn't really discussed that," Hal answered as he looked at Sharon. "I have some business commitments coming up, though, so it probably won't be until July. How about a trip around the 4th?" he asked Sharon.

"Oh, that would be terrific," Sharon replied, smiling.

She'd been hoping they could meet more frequently, but she realized it wasn't entirely fair to expect him to travel to her more often if she wasn't reciprocating. Still, she wondered how a long-distance relationship would work. Mandy seemed to be happier about this turn of events, however.

*She's probably hoping that means this won't last,* Sharon thought somewhat petulantly as she noticed Mandy's expression and realized she was not happy about the reactions both by Mandy and her. This was something they'd need to talk about after Hal left.

The rest of the meal went as well as Sharon had expected, even though she'd hoped it would have turned out better. It was still asking too much to think that Mandy could suddenly switch her feelings off as close as she had been with Tom, though.

*I just need to give her more time.*

She hoped that was all it would be as she wasn't ready to break off the relationship with Hal, but she didn't want to alienate Mandy either. Relationships were rarely easy when blending families, but should one person's happiness exclude another's if it meant giving up someone who they wanted to be with? That was a question that would remain to be answered and would not happen today, so no point obsessing over it.

"It was nice to meet you, Hal," Jessica told him. "I guess we'll see you again in July."

"Really nice to meet you, too," Hal answered. "I'm looking forward to seeing both of you again," he said as he made a point of looking at Mandy.

Mandy smiled, but only with her lips and it was clear that she was doing so only to be polite.

"I guess we'll see what happens between now and then," was all she said.

Sharon held her tongue but added that to her mental list of things to discuss with Mandy later.

They all said their final goodbyes, and Sharon and Hal headed home.

"You're quiet," Hal said after they'd been driving a few miles.

"Oh, sorry, I was just replaying the evening in my head. I really was hoping Mandy would be more gracious."

"I noticed a bit of an undertone of disapproval," Hal responded wryly.

"That's how I took it, too," Sharon affirmed. "I'm going to have a talk with her after you leave. I really don't want this to be a thing between us."

"It's going to take some time, Sharon. She's not a child, but her emotions are still raw and everyone has their own pace for how they grieve."

"I know, and I guess I should just give it more time. I can't make her like you and that's not what I'm trying to do," she added, "but I hoped that for my sake she'd at least try a little harder to put her own feelings aside."

"What's that expression, it's a process. This one may be a multi-step process but hopefully not quite as many steps as it took Edison to invent the light bulb."

Sharon laughed.

"I hope not, too," she replied, and felt better. Her mood was not as heavy as when they'd left the restaurant. "I really want our last night together to be happy, so I promise you I'm letting this go and my focus is entirely on you."

He reached over and stroked her hair, which gave her comfort, and she looked over and smiled at him.

"I'm glad you came into my life," she said.

"Me, too," he responded. "We can make this work."

"I hope so. It will be work but I'm willing to give it my best."

They spent their last night together making plans for Hal's return in July and their lovemaking was bittersweet, knowing that Hal would be leaving and that it would be more than two months before they would see each other again.

* * *

HAL HAD CHOSEN the early flight out so they were up well before dawn in order to have him at the airport by 4:30 AM.

"Thank you for coming this week. I'm going to miss you," Sharon told him as they said their goodbyes at the airport.

"It was my pleasure. I'm going to miss you, too," he said before kissing her in a way that let her know she would be missed.

"You're going to make me cry and I do not want to do that," she admonished him, knowing he would realize her emotions were running high.

"I don't want to make you cry, either. It's just two months and we'll be talking to each other. This isn't a farewell, it's just an until later."

"I know, and I'm being silly. It will be fine," she said and straightened up as though to enforce that statement as much for herself as for him.

They kissed one last time before he picked up his carryon and walked into the terminal. Sharon watched him for a moment before getting back into her car and heading back home. A tear rolled down her cheek, and she brushed it away absentmindedly.

*It's going to be fine*, she thought. *Then why do I feel so insecure about this?*

No answer came.

# CHAPTER EIGHT

Sharon debated whether to go back to bed but decided it would just make her feel worse. A nap later in the afternoon might not be off the agenda, though. It was too early to call the girls and too chilly to work in the yard, so to keep herself from wandering aimlessly through the house, she got her iPad to read but found herself rereading the same paragraph over and over again. Giving up, she went back to bed and was surprised to find that she had been more tired than she realized when she woke up at 7:30. She knew Mandy was an early riser, and she wanted to clear the air with her sooner than later, so texted first to see if she was up and could do a FaceTime call. She wanted to see Mandy's expressions and body language rather than just hear her voice while they talked.

**Are you up for a FaceTime call?** she typed and hit Send before setting up the coffeemaker. She hadn't had any earlier just in case she had been able to get back to sleep.

She heard the tone alerting her a FaceTime call was coming through and clicked on.

"Good morning," Mandy announced. "You're up early."

"I had to get Hal to the airport for his 6 AM flight, so was up very early. I went back to bed when I got home, though, so getting up for the second time today. You must have been up early yourself. That didn't take any time at all for you to call me back," Sharon said, and smiled.

"It's habit by now. I get up so early during the week to go into the office that sleeping until 7 feels like sleeping in," Mandy smiled back.

"I wanted to talk to you about last night," Sharon started hesitantly and frowned from concern rather than anger.

Mandy sighed.

"I was sort of expecting a call from you about that," she said. "Mom, I hope you know I am trying, but this is still really raw for me and I couldn't keep my emotions as much under control as I'd hoped. That was me being welcoming."

"I do appreciate what you're going through, but I would have hated to see what your not welcoming attitude would have been." She could see from Mandy's expression that things could take a downturn, so quickly added, "But I didn't call to give you grief about it. I was hoping we could talk this out like adults and to let you know I want to take your feelings into account, too."

"Thanks, Mom," Mandy said softly. She sighed again and took a breath before speaking. "I want you to know that I want you to be happy and if that means being with someone new, I'll try to not get in the way of that. But…."

"Uh, oh, I had a feeling there would be a but coming," Sharon tried to keep her voice teasing and the mood light.

"But…." Mandy continued. "I have a bad feeling about Hal. I can't quite put my finger on it but there's something too…. maybe smarmy is the word I'm struggling for."

"Did you actually say smarmy?!" Sharon laughed. "I didn't know you even knew that word."

"Must have heard it from you," Mandy teased.

"So you took what I see as charm being too over the top?"

Sharon asked in what she hoped Mandy understood was her attempt to make sure she was on the same page.

"Yeah, it didn't come across as charming at all to me. It was like he was trying too hard, and it just rubbed me the wrong way. It feels like he's hiding something instead. I don't mean it in a way that I think he's some sort of con man trying to empty your bank accounts, but I still don't trust him. The last thing I want to happen to you is to get hurt and I'm afraid that's exactly what's going to happen with him."

Sharon nodded as she considered what to say next.

"Thank you and I mean that sincerely. I don't want to get hurt either, but I think this is something I have to follow to see how it goes. It may end up that we find out we're not at all right for each other. I like him a lot and I hope it doesn't but I'm enough of a realist to know that possibility is there. Long-distance relationships are difficult under the best of circumstances, if there is such a thing as best circumstances, and that may be what kills this one. I promise I'll keep your feelings and advice in mind, though, and proceed with caution. Would that make you feel better?"

"It's all I can ask," Mandy told her.

"Thanks, honey. You know I love you and you and Jess will always be my first priority, right?"

"I do."

"Well, good, now that we've got the heavy stuff out of the way, what's on your agenda for the rest of the day?"

They spent a few more minutes chatting before agreeing to meet up later in the day and asking Jessica to join them for lunch.

## CHAPTER NINE

It had been a few days since Sharon had spoken with Donna, so called her later that afternoon after getting home from lunch with the girls.

"Well, hey, stranger," Donna announced upon picking up the call.

"I realized it had been a few days, and you were on my mind. What have you been up to?"

"Not much other than trying to keep the new neighbor on my right from pestering me," Donna replied.

"Uh oh, are you going to need to speak to the HOA?" Sharon asked. "What is he, or is it a she, doing to pester you?"

"It's a he and I can't decide if he's just obtuse or persistent. I'm not sure how many different ways I can say I'm not interested in more than a passing hello if we happen to see each other without being downright rude before he takes the hint."

Sharon laughed. "Sounds like you've got your own Mr. Baggy Pants," she teased. This was an inside joke between the two of them regarding a gentleman in their gourd class who'd fancied himself as a Casanova.

"Oh, my word, you've hit the nail on the head," Donna

agreed. "I mean, he seems like a nice enough person, but culti-vating a male friendship is not something that's of any interest whatsoever to me at the moment. I've still got divorce scars heal-ing, and that's the last thing I want in my life right now!"

"You have my complete confidence that you'll be able to get that across, no matter how obtuse or persistent he is," Sharon declared.

"When does Hal come to see you? Or has he already been there? I've forgotten when you told me he was coming."

"He's been here already. I dropped him off at the airport this morning for his 6 AM flight back to Tucson."

"You must have been up before daylight! How did it go? Did he meet the girls? Did they like him?"

Sharon laughed at the rapid-fire questions.

"It went well with Hal and me. Yes, he met the girls. The verdict is still out on whether they liked him. I think it's safe to say that Jess is still on the fence, but unless I ask her point blank will probably keep that to herself. Mandy, on the other hand, is not impressed but doing her best to let me make my own choices."

"How are you with that?" Donna asked.

"I'm okay, at least with accepting that her feelings are her feelings and she's an adult who has opinions about wanting me to not get hurt. She mentioned, though, that she doesn't trust Hal and is worried that he's a bit of a con man. Not in the taking me for my money sense, but she doesn't completely trust his good intentions. I'm not sure I'm explaining that right, but do you know what I mean?"

"I think so," Donna replied. "Is she afraid you're rushing into the relationship?"

"Oh, definitely!" Sharon agreed. "At first it was about her feelings that I was doing this so close to when Tom died, but after she met Hal, she said it was more of a feeling she had about him. She actually used the word smarmy!"

Donna laughed before asking, "How do you feel about it?"

Sharon considered before answering.

"It's definitely playing into my guilt that maybe I am rushing things, but on the other hand, I want to give it a chance. I'll try to be philosophical about it if it doesn't work out, but I'm in a little too deep already to say I won't get hurt if it ends up being just a fling."

"That sounds like the best attitude. Life sometimes means taking risks."

"Deep advice from the lady who doesn't even want to say more than hello to her new neighbor," Sharon teased.

"You got me on that one. I'm going to stick to do as I say, not as I do, though."

"And on that note, I'll let you go. It was great to hear your voice. I miss our weekly get-togethers!" Sharon told her.

"Me, too. I can't wait for you to get back. Keep me posted on how it goes with Hal and Mandy."

"Will do," Sharon promised, and they said their goodbyes.

# CHAPTER TEN

It wasn't long before Sharon settled back into the routine of life in Maine. The days grew warmer, and she could spend time in her gardens. They had taken a back burner the past couple of years between her day job and caring for Tom, but now that she was retired, she could give them the attention they deserved. She and Hal had kept the romance alive, and the time had finally arrived for him to return for a visit as he'd promised for the Fourth of July holiday. He'd be spending two weeks this time now that there would be better weather for exploring the Maine coastline and they'd talked about spending a couple of days in the Boston area as well, with an option for an extended trip to Cape Cod. Sharon was hoping that Mandy would have had enough time to get used to the idea that Hal's presence in her life wasn't going away anytime soon. They'd be getting together for a barbeque to celebrate the Fourth, so she'd soon find out.

Sharon glanced at her watch and was surprised to see that it was nearly time for her to go to the airport to pick up Hal. He'd taken the earlier flight this time, so would arrive around 5:30 and she'd planned a light dinner that was already prepped and ready.

She checked his flight for its ETA to make sure it was on schedule and then headed upstairs for a quick shower to freshen up after working in the garden, and then she'd be good to go.

Her phone chimed, announcing Hal's text that they'd landed and were taxiing into the terminal area. Thinking she'd have time to check her emails while she was waiting, it startled her to hear the tap on the passenger side window. She looked up, surprised to see Hal smiling at her instead of airport security telling her to move her vehicle. She smiled back and unlocked the doors so he could get in.

"Do you have another bag?" she asked, seeing that all he had was the carryon. "I'd expected you'd be a few more minutes waiting for Baggage Claim."

"I'm a light packer," he replied. "I figured I could do laundry at your house if you don't mind so I wouldn't have to bother checking a bag."

"No, of course, that's no problem at all. It didn't even occur to me although I don't know why. It's so good to finally see you in person again."

"I've missed you, too. This was even harder than I thought it would be but I'm here now, for the next two weeks at least."

"I wish it was longer," Sharon said as she glanced over at him.

"Maybe we can talk about that," Hal suggested.

"Oh?" she asked, almost forgetting to check the traffic before pulling out, she was so surprised.

"I don't have any jobs coming up in the next month that would require me to be at home and if you wouldn't mind my using your internet and being preoccupied for a few hours at a time, I could still do the jobs I'm working on from here."

"That would be wonderful!" she exclaimed. "Yet another thing it never occurred to me to mention before. I guess I just assumed you'd have to be in either Tucson or Minnesota more often and didn't want to ask you to make special arrangements."

"You never think of yourself first, do you?" Hal asked.

Sharon thought that over before answering.

"I guess you're mostly right. I have spent a lot of my life putting others before myself. To be honest, being with you may be one of the first times I didn't overthink whether I should be thinking more about anyone else's feelings."

"Are there still reservations from Mandy about us?"

"I suspect there may be. She hasn't really said much since you were here the last time, but when I invited her over for the barbeque on the Fourth, I sensed some negativity below the surface. And, by the way, I didn't have a chance to let you know that there will be more of us as Jess and Mandy will both be bringing their boyfriends."

"That could be a good thing, as she might be more likely to be on best behavior and not cause any scenes," Hal responded.

"I hope you're right."

# CHAPTER ELEVEN

The Fourth of July was a perfect summer day with nearly cloudless skies and the temperatures forecast to be in the mid-80s but low humidity. Sharon had told Jessica and Amanda to come over any time after 3 PM and that she had everything under control as far as food was concerned.

Jessica and her boyfriend, Scott Dalton, arrived first. They had been high school sweethearts but had parted company when Scott went out of state to attend college. He'd returned after graduation and was teaching English at a local high school, but they'd only recently reconnected and from the chemistry she saw between them, Sharon wouldn't be surprised if they made an engagement announcement soon. She knew Jess would like to have children and had just recently turned 30 which was not old by current standards, but she had let Sharon know she might give up on the idea if she wasn't in a serious relationship soon.

After introducing Hal and Scott, they went to the deck to have a beer while Sharon and Jess began preparations for dinner. There really wasn't much to do since Sharon had made the potato salad earlier that day and the burgers were formed and in the fridge until it was time to get them on the grill.

"It's good to see Scott again. You both look very happy with each other," Sharon tried to act casual as she got out the paper plates and utensils.

"Smooth, Mom," Jess laughed as the unasked question hung in the air.

"You mean I wasn't as subtle as I thought I was?" Sharon asked, knowing the answer.

"Um, no. And to answer what you're really asking, yes, we have been talking about marriage and are definitely heading in that direction, but nothing has been set in stone, or more specifically, a diamond, so don't go making any wedding plans yet."

"Roger. Got that loud and clear," she laughed, letting Jess know she wasn't upset.

"Sorry, I hope that didn't come out too harshly." Jess seemed embarrassed.

Jessica was always the peacemaker and never the one to cause any outbursts or confrontations, so Sharon gave her a big hug to let her know there was no need to worry about how she'd reacted to Jess's remarks.

"Have you heard from Mandy today?" Sharon asked.

"She texted just before we got here and said she and Mike were on their way and should be here in about a half hour."

"I hope this time will be different. She wasn't so much rude to Hal last time he was here as just not overly friendly, but I know it was still a shock for her to find out I'd begun dating. Maybe by now she's had time to adjust. Has she talked to you about it at all?"

"No," Jess replied, "but I get the feeling she may have been hoping this would blow over because of the long-distance piece."

They heard a knock on the door just before it opened, and Mandy and Mike walked in carrying a box and a bottle of wine.

"We brought some fireworks for later," Mike announced. "I hope that's okay."

"Nothing too loud, I hope," Sharon replied with a slight

frown. "If there is such a thing when it comes to fireworks. There are a few dogs in the neighborhood and oftentimes, the noise can be terrifying for them."

"I don't think these should be too bad," Mike reassured her, "but we don't have to light them off if that's a problem."

"Mom, really, you don't have to be such a killjoy," Mandy told her.

"I'm not trying to, but you remember how scared Cindy used to get, don't you?"

They'd had a black Lab when the girls were growing up and thunderstorms and fireworks had always terrified her. She would spend the entire time shivering and trying to be in someone's lap despite her size until the noise finally stopped.

"Yeah, I guess you're right. I had forgotten about that. Are there still dogs in the neighborhood, though?"

"The Russells have a Golden. I don't know if she's scared about loud noises, but I've just tried to be considerate and never put it to the test."

She saw the look on Mandy's face and realized her remark may have come out more harshly than she'd intended.

"Why don't we grab drinks for you two and go out on the deck so I can introduce Mike. Hal and Scott are already out there. What can I get you?"

They each asked for a beer for now, and they all headed out to the deck. Hal and Scott stood up to greet them.

Before Sharon could make the introductions, Hal extended his hand to Mike. "Hi, I'm Hal Jackson and you are?"

"Michael Wilson, but you can call me Mike," he said as he shook Hal's hand.

"Mandy, it's good to see you again. I hope we can get to know each other better this time now that I'll be here longer."

"How long before you go back?" Mandy's tone was brusque and Sharon gave her a look of warning.

"I'll be here two weeks, but your mom and I were discussing

the possibility of my coming back again soon and staying for a more extended time."

Mandy looked at Sharon as though hoping she would dispute the announcement, but Sharon only shook her head in agreement with Hal's statement. Sharon's stomach knotted, fearing that this could get out of control soon if they did not bring things back to another topic.

Jess interjected, as though also sensing the change in mood, "How is work going, Mike? I heard you have a big case coming up."

Mike was a lawyer in another firm in Bangor than the one where Mandy worked. They had met in law school and he had applied for the position although his family was from Massachusetts, after it looked like their relationship was going to continue even after they'd graduated.

"It is. I can't say much about it since we'll be going to trial soon, but it could be a big one for my career. I'll still have to pay my dues as an associate, but the partners will be looking to see how I do, and it could bump me up on the promotion list if it turns out in our favor."

"Well, good luck. I hope it turns out for you," Sharon told him.

Mandy was quiet and had seemed to withdraw into herself, but Sharon had learned that it was best to let her process her feelings on her own rather than focusing on them, so didn't try to draw her into the conversations. If she didn't start participating after another half hour, she decided she would ask her to help her alone in the kitchen so she could have a talk with her. She didn't want the day to be uncomfortable for anyone and it was becoming more obvious as time went on that Mandy was too quiet to just be politely letting others talk. Just as she thought she'd have to do that, Mandy came out of her self-imposed silence and join the others as they got to know each other, or at least how Hal fit into their group.

They shared laughs and conversation as well as a traditional New England Fourth of July meal of hamburgers and hot dogs on the grill, corn on the cob, potato salad, and strawberry short-cake for dessert. Mandy had seemed to be doing better and had even been laughing and taking part in conversations with Hal. After some discussion, they decided to forego the fireworks that Mike had brought out of consideration for any animals in the neighborhood that might not appreciate the celebration. Hal and Sharon turned down the invitation to go into Bangor to watch the fireworks there and said their goodbyes to the others.

"Well, that didn't go too bad," Hal said as he helped Sharon clean up the last of the dishes and put away the remaining food.

"I admit I was holding my breath for a while, but Mandy got over herself," Sharon agreed.

"So, I take it I still haven't won her over?" Hal asked.

"Let's say the jury is still out. I knew it would take some time but had hoped she'd warmed up to you. At least by the end of the evening she seemed to be less…. hostile isn't exactly the word I'd use…"

"Oh, I think that would work," he teased.

"Yeah, you may be right," Sharon conceded.

He took her in his arms and looked into her eyes. "We'll be okay. You know that, right?"

"I hope so," Sharon told him.

"It's a little early, but what do you say we call it a night," he asked as he gave her a kiss and then took her hand and led her upstairs, knowing she'd have no objection.

* * *

OVER THE NEXT couple of weeks, they took several day trips to places they hadn't been able to visit on his last trip to Maine and made plans for Hal to return in another couple of weeks for an extended stay so that they could decide if the relationship could transition from feeling things out to committed. They'd agreed to be monogamous not long after they'd begun dating, but there'd never been an understanding that this would be more than temporary.

"How long do you think you'll need in Minnesota?" Sharon asked.

"Not long," Hal answered as he continued packing his suitcase for his return trip the next morning. "I want to make sure my house is buttoned up and will need to make sure the mail gets forwarded here. You're sure it's okay?"

"Of course."

"There probably wouldn't be much since most of my correspondence is done by email these days and all my bills are set up on auto-pay but there might be some client work that would come through and I don't want to miss any of that if it's a project I'm not currently working on."

"Really, it's no problem at all," Sharon smiled reassuringly.

"And are you sure about this?" he asked.

She knew he meant sharing her house. There hadn't been any more outbursts from Mandy, but they hadn't had that many interactions either and it was as though Sharon was waiting for the other shoe to drop. She'd never had to do the blended household since the girls were so young when she had first started dating Tom.

"I am. I can't promise that there won't still be some objections from the peanut gallery but we're all adults here so I'm hoping we can discuss it and work it out if there are."

"Okay, then," he replied as though crossing that off his mental to do list and finished up his packing. "I'll just need to add my toiletries in the morning but otherwise I'm all set."

"I feel a lot better about you leaving this time. At least I know you'll be back soon. I really missed you a lot last time."

"I missed you, too. More than I thought I would, which was a lot," he added as he saw the look of disappointment on Sharon's face. "It's why I wanted to take this next step and suggested we spend more time together to see if this can work long term."

"It's a big step," Sharon agreed. "I don't know that I would have brought it up even though it's what I would have liked to happen. I guess I'm still a little old-fashioned about waiting to be asked."

"I've noticed. I had a feeling I'd have to be the one to make the first move. Maybe we can work on that, though. It's okay for you to be more assertive with me, you know."

"Really?" she teased. "So you wouldn't mind if I told you I want to make love with you… now… and I want to be in charge."

"Whoa! Where did that come from?" Hal smiled and didn't seem the least bit unhappy about Sharon's change in direction. "Not that I'm complaining at all. In fact, I really like this new take charge Sharon."

"Then fasten your seat belt, this may be a bumpy ride."

She walked over to him and kissed him with an intensity she'd never shown him before, exploring his tongue with hers and running her hand across his chest and down to unfasten his jeans. She slapped his hand lightly as he tried to help.

"I'm in charge," she told him.

"Yes, ma'am," he replied, smiling as he did.

She took his hand and led him to the bed and showed him exactly how in charge she was.

* * *

HAL HAD CHOSEN the early flight out again for the next day, so it was another night of very little sleep for them both.

They kissed goodbye at the airport with promises to call or text as soon as he arrived home.

"See you soon."

"See you soon. I love you." Sharon's hand went to her mouth

as though to try to put the words back in. "I didn't mean to say that. It just came out."

He kissed her again. "No need to apologize. I think I love you, too."

They hugged for longer than they might otherwise have before he broke the embrace with one last kiss before heading inside the terminal.

"Well, that was unexpected," Sharon said out loud and then realized what she'd done, but there was no one to hear her, so no need to feel embarrassed as she got into her car to head back home.

# CHAPTER TWELVE

Sharon woke the next morning feeling younger than she had in years. After her revelation to Hal, and just as much to herself, of how she felt about him, it was as though a new chapter of her life was about to begin. How that would play out remained to be seen. He had called when he got back to his house, and they had talked about when he could come back to Maine and for how long. They'd decided four to six weeks might be a good start to figure out how this would go. Spending a couple of weeks together had worked out well, but it was more like being on vacation with someone than living with them and sharing daily life and all that brought with it. In other words, would they be able to make it past the honeymoon phase? Sharon had a lot to do here as well. Hal would need an office area, but she could rearrange one of the spare bedrooms as it was unlikely that she'd need it. It was a four-bedroom house and she'd thought about downsizing, especially after Tom's death, but had put it off heeding the advice of not making any big decisions for the first year following the death of a loved one. She'd already ignored that advice by jumping into a new relationship.

*It just happened.* Sharon realized she was justifying her

behavior to herself but dismissed the feeling. She really didn't want to heed that piece of advice right now when she was feeling so happy about it.

Hal had realized it would only take him a few days to put affairs in order, since most things could be accomplished online these days. The biggest necessities for the longer stay were to have more clothes and a car, so would drive instead of flying back to Maine.

The phone rang, interrupting Sharon's cleaning and rearranging of the spare room.

"Hi, Jess," she answered, seeing Jessica's name come up on her caller ID.

"Hi, Mom. What are you up to today?" Jess asked.

"Well, for the moment, I'm cleaning the spare room and trying to arrange things so that Hal can use it as an office while he's here. He'll be back on Friday, so I have a few days, but I thought I'd try to get it done now. What about you, any plans for the day?"

"Hal will be back already?" she asked.

"Yes, we decided we'd try spending longer together as we'd mentioned yesterday, and this seemed as good a time as any to do that."

"It sounds like things are getting more serious," Jess said, more of a question than a statement.

"I think it might be, but that's what we'll have to find out. How do you feel about that?"

"Honestly, Mom, I don't know. I want you to be happy…"

"But?"

"I don't know. It just feels… off…" Jess finished, her voice trailing off.

"And here I thought it was Mandy I would need to be worrying about."

Sharon sat down at the desk she'd been dusting, and her good mood started to slip away.

"You don't need to worry about my feelings," Jess reassured her. "I know this is something you have to figure out for yourself, and I don't want to stand in your way. Not that that's what I'm trying to do."

"I'm guessing you're worried I might get hurt and how well do I really know Hal, is that about right?"

"Yeah, that's it," Jess agreed.

"I really appreciate that you feel that way, although I do feel a little like our roles have been reversed," Sharon chuckled. "I'll be okay, honey. I'm a big girl and it might be a mistake, but I'll never know unless I give it a try. Now, back to my original question, what's on your agenda today?"

Jess seemed as happy to be changing the subject as Sharon was and let it drop.

"I was thinking of checking out that new shop downtown that sells locally made crafts and wondered if you'd like to join me? Maybe we could grab a bite to eat, too."

"That's a great idea! I've been wanting to check that out myself and had just never made the time to do it. Should I just meet you there and what time?"

"How about going for lunch first and then we can check out that store and some of the other ones downtown. It's been a while since I've looked around and I think there may be a couple of new shops since I was there the last time. Would you be able to make it around 11? There's a new restaurant on Central Street called Farm Fresh that's supposed to be good."

"Sounds like a plan. See you then."

Sharon went back to putting the spare room in order. She checked her watch and saw that more time had gone by than she'd thought. She realized she would need to get ready soon to meet Jess and would have to finish the organizing later. It wouldn't take her long to drive to the restaurant, but parking could be difficult downtown, so she wanted to give herself some extra time. As it turned out, she arrived with time to spare and got a table so they wouldn't need to wait once Jessica arrived. It came as a surprise when not just Jessica, but Amanda also showed up.

"Mandy, how nice to see you, too!"

"It occurred to me that we haven't done just a girls' day in a long time, so I asked her if she'd like to join us. I hope that was okay," Jessica said.

"Of course! It was a great idea and you're right, it's been too long since we've done this."

Sharon began to feel like this was not as much of an afterthought as Jessica was trying to make it sound when she saw the determined expressions on both their faces. The server showed up then to ask for their drink orders and they told her they would need a few more minutes to make their meal choices. Once she'd left to get the drinks, Sharon's suspicions were confirmed.

"Mom, are you serious? You're actually going to have Hal come to live with you? I mean, I know you said that, but I guess I thought you couldn't possibly be serious," Mandy sprung on her.

"Yes, I'm serious, and no, he's not coming to live with me. At least not yet. This is a trial to see if we're ready to take that next step. And I would hope that you two would stop treating me as though I have no sense at all and am about to get played."

She hadn't wanted this to become confrontational, especially out in a public setting, but her patience was wearing thin. Jessica was visibly uncomfortable, but Mandy looked as though she was just getting started. Her training as a lawyer might have been kicking in, but Sharon did not appreciate being on the receiving end of feeling as though she was being put on trial.

"I know you don't like Hal, Mandy. You're making that abundantly clear, but could you please let me be the judge of whether or not I'm able to handle myself? I haven't stepped into assisted living status quite yet."

Mandy seemed to take this to heart, and her expression softened.

"I'm sorry, Mom, you're right. It's not that I don't like Hal. He has some wonderful qualities, I'm sure, but there's something about him I just don't trust. I can't put my finger on what it is."

"Well, maybe this is exactly what you need, too. You haven't really spent a lot of time around him, so his being here for a longer time could be just what you need to get to know him better. Maybe then you could see him the way I do. There has been nothing so far that he's said or done that would make me doubt I should trust him and he's always treated me well."

Mandy hesitated, but Sharon gave her the time to consider.

"Okay, you win. I'll try but you know I'm going to be honest with you if I don't change my mind."

"That you'll try is all I can ask. Well, no, I can and am going to ask that you not be rude. I don't need to be on pins and needles whenever you're around each other, waiting for something to happen. At least give it a fair chance and try to stay open-minded. Maybe you're judging him unfairly because you haven't come to grips with losing your dad and feeling like Hal is an interloper."

"I don't think that's it," Mandy answered somewhat defensively, "but for you I'll try to put my feelings aside and give him a chance."

Just then, the server showed up with their drinks and they asked for just another few minutes to look over the menu. The discussion was dropped, and although they were able to move on to spend the next few hours together for their girls' day, there was an undercurrent of expectation that this was not over.

# CHAPTER THIRTEEN

"*A*re you going somewhere?"

Hal's expression and tone stopped Sharon in her tracks. It had been a month since he'd arrived back in Maine and until now, things had been going fine. There were concessions, of course, as they each got used to being around each other 24/7, but it had been an amiable adjustment.

"I was just coming to let you know I was going shopping," she answered. "Jess's birthday is in a couple weeks so I wanted to see if I could find her a present."

"How long will you be gone?"

"Probably a couple hours, maybe a little longer," Sharon hesitated before going on, not sure which direction to take this. "I'm sorry, but are you saying I should be asking for permission?" her own tone taking on a defensive posture.

Hal's expression changed, perhaps realizing he'd gone too far.

"No, of course not," he smiled as though to reassure her.

"I hope not, Hal," her tone serious. "Tom and I had an understanding that although we were a couple, we each had separate interests. We let each other know what we were doing or where we were going out of courtesy, so I guess it never occurred to me that you might have had a different understanding with your ex."

"Of course, of course." Hal walked toward her to give her a hug. "I'm sorry that came out the way it did. This project I'm working on is giving me some problems, but I shouldn't have taken it out on you."

She hugged him back, but found she was not as relieved as she might have been.

"Apology accepted," she replied. "Maybe some space is just what we both need. We've pretty much been with each other constantly since you came back. I'm finding it's not as easy to be with someone all the time as I had thought it would be and it sounds like that may be true for you as well."

"I think you're right. You're the first person I've ever lived with since my divorce and that was three years ago."

"We've never talked about your divorce," Sharon said, realizing for the first time that this topic had never been broached.

"I didn't think we needed to," Hal answered. "It was in the past, and I'd moved on. We had just grown apart and the official grounds were the usual these days… irreconcilable differences."

"Yes, that does seem to be term."

Sharon considered whether this was the time to pursue this further but decided against it. She wasn't certain if that had more to do with wanting to put this behind them quickly or that she really wanted to leave to find Jess's birthday present.

"Well, I'll leave you to your project and hope it goes more smoothly," she said, giving him a quick kiss and hug.

He hugged her one more time before releasing her. "Thanks, and I hope you find the perfect present. Have fun!"

"Thanks, on both counts,' she smiled back and left on her shopping mission.

Sharon was still unsettled as she drove away, trying to put her finger on just what had made her feel so uncomfortable.

"Ahh, that's it," she said aloud as it came to her. This was exactly how her first husband had treated her. He had been, probably still was, a control freak and although the relationship had never become physically abusive, his constant demands to know where she was at all times and attempts to isolate her from friends and family had finally driven her to ask for a divorce. It had been contentious, especially because Jessica and Amanda were in the picture, but she'd always been thankful that the divorce had gone through before they'd become a domestic abuse statistic. And then she'd met Tom and their lives had turned around and those memories of her first marriage had long been buried. She considered whether this really was the same, since Hal had never treated her like this before. He did have a reason for his behavior, but all the same, her history told her she should be more alert for red flags that might come up.

# CHAPTER FOURTEEN

The next couple of weeks had gone by with no more arguments and Sharon had put it behind her, thinking Hal's explanation had been the truth that he was out of sorts because of the project he'd been working on. They were hosting the girls and their boyfriends that evening for Jessica's birthday celebration, and she'd been looking forward to it. There had been a truce of sorts between Hal and Mandy, so it came as a complete surprise to her when Mandy had asked Hal how much longer he was going to be here. It wasn't so much the words as the tone Mandy had used that had put her on alert that this could go badly.

"I'm heading back next week," Hal said as he smiled at Mandy, ignoring the confrontational tone she'd used.

"You what?" Sharon asked in total surprise. "You hadn't said anything about this."

"I thought we didn't need to ask permission," he smiled at her, but she could see the smile did not reach his eyes. "I was planning to let you know later this evening, but Mandy forced my hand."

"I see," she responded. "Well, in that case, we can have that conversation later. Right now, this is about Jess," she smiled in Jess's direction, "so let's celebrate." She finished and looked at Mandy, warning her without words to drop any more attempts to cause an argument.

It took a few minutes, but the mood changed, and everyone was able to enjoy the rest of the evening. They had a lovely dinner, her favorite chocolate cake for dessert, followed by opening her birthday gifts. Jess made a point of buying locally sourced items, and Sharon had found the perfect pair of earrings made by one of Jess's favorite Maine artisans during her shopping trip. It was an early evening since it was a weekday when everyone left to go home.

"Is now a good time to have that conversation about you leaving?" Sharon asked, despite not wanting to bring it up after having seen Hal's expression earlier.

"Sure. Look, I'm sorry it came out the way it did, but Mandy took me by surprise. "

"When were you planning to tell me?"

"Like I said, I was going to tell you either tonight or tomorrow," he replied, and she could see he was becoming defensive.

"What brought this on?" Sharon asked. "I didn't know you were even thinking about it."

"I think we need a little break," he said as he held her shoulders and looked into her eyes. "This has been a huge adjustment for both of us and I don't want things to snowball. Plus, I have some things I need to take care of back home in Minnesota and from there I'm going back to Tucson. I want this to work, Sharon, and right now I think the best way to make sure that happens is to give us a little space."

"I see," she replied, looking away and fighting back tears.

"Don't cry," he said as he pulled her into an embrace and stroked the back of her hair.

She bit her lip, willing herself not to cry. He'd told her this wasn't a breakup, and maybe they did just need a time out. In some ways, the news came as a relief, and she realized she needed some space as well.

"How about if you come back to Arizona?" he asked.

"I hadn't decided for sure if I wanted to go back that early," she answered. "I really want to be here for the holidays."

"You could always fly back here for the holidays," he suggested.

"Yeah, I guess that would work," she considered. "I've always wondered what Arizona is like in autumn. It's always a bit depressing here for me that time of year once it's gotten too cold to be outside."

"There you go, it's settled then?" he asked.

"Maybe," she smiled up at him. "Let me think about it a little more, but I'm giving it serious consideration."

"That's all I can ask."

"When will you be leaving?" she asked, but not feeling as afraid to hear the answer as she had been earlier.

"I was thinking the day after tomorrow."

"So soon?" she asked, her voice trembling despite herself.

"Like I said, I have some things I need to take care of and with having to drive back this time, I'll need a few extra days than if I'd flown."

"Of course, it's just that I'm going to miss you. I know we need this break but it's still going to be strange to not have you here."

"For me, too, but I think it's best in the long run."

"I hope so," she whispered.

They made love slowly and tenderly and fell asleep wrapped in each other's arms.

# CHAPTER FIFTEEN

It had been a week since Hal left to go back to Minnesota and then on to Tucson. Sharon had thought over the proposal to go back to Arizona. She had considered that as a possibility before she'd returned to Maine in the spring, but it hadn't been set in stone. The more she thought about it, though, the more she realized that was what she wanted to do. Coming back for the holidays would take some planning, but if it worked out, this might be how she would do this from now on.

"I have something I want to let you know," she announced to the girls over dinner.

Mandy's face looked panic-stricken, and Sharon had to laugh.

"No, Hal and I are not getting married," she told her, anticipating what Mandy's panic had meant.

"Oh, thank goodness," Mandy exhaled in relief, much to Sharon's annoyance, but she let it pass.

"You may not like this news any better," she decided to say rather than picking at the other thread. "I've decided I'm going to go back to Arizona at the end of the month. I'll come back for the holidays," she added quickly, seeing the look on both girls' faces. "I wouldn't want to miss either Thanksgiving or Christmas with either of you, but I would like to see what it's like there this time of year and it's also a long time to leave the house there unattended."

"Don't you have someone looking after it while you're here, just like you do for this house?" Jess asked.

"I do. Joseph recommended someone in the area who does that sort of thing, but I just need to get back," Sharon finished lamely, realizing she wasn't putting this into words well. She wasn't sure if it was because she was making excuses to herself or to them but feeling upset as well that she was being asked to justify her reasons as though she were a child.

"Does this have to do with Hal, or is this really your idea?" Mandy asked.

"I admit he suggested it but it was something I'd been thinking over myself, just not as seriously until he brought it up."

"Just as I figured," Mandy replied in a sarcastic tone.

"I don't need attitude," Sharon reprimanded. "I'm an adult and I don't really need your permission, but I would like you to be okay with this."

"Mom," Jess interjected, hoping to cool the mood, "Of course, it's up to you. We're just going to miss you, aren't we, Mandy?"

"That's not what this is about, Jess, and you know that. Just because you're too afraid to say anything to Mom's face about it, doesn't mean I don't know you don't think it's a good idea either."

Jessica's face turned red, and she looked down at her hands, avoiding Sharon's questioning gaze.

"Jess, is there something you'd like to tell me?" she asked.

Jess took a deep breath, settling herself before responding to Sharon.

"Mom, you know I love you and I'm not going to stand in your way, but I hope you're not making a mistake with Hal. I thought at first that Mandy was making a big deal about him. I admit I wasn't thrilled about the idea that you were dating someone so soon after Dad died, but that happens sometimes. I was willing to give him a chance for your sake, but I don't know...." she trailed off.

Sharon didn't know what to make of this. She'd taken Amanda's objections with a grain of salt and had expected them because of her closeness to Tom, but she hadn't expected it from Jessica. This put a different spin on things.

They all sat in silence for a few minutes as each of them considered what to say next. Sharon broke the silence first.

"I want both of you to know that I love you with all my heart, and I hope you don't think I am being dismissive of your feelings. But... perhaps this is exactly what I need to do right now and knowing how you both feel about Hal, I promise I will keep that in my mind before making any long-term decisions about where our relationship goes. I'm going to go to Arizona and will be back for the holidays just as I said, but with my eyes wide open. I hope you can both be okay with that."

Mandy and Jess exchanged glances in silent communication before speaking.

"I won't say I'm happy about it," Mandy was the first to speak, "but I hear what you're saying and you're right. If that's what you need to do to make a decision, it's your life and I have no right to keep you from doing that."

"What she said," Jess smiled, in her usual way of trying to have everyone get along.

Sharon got up to give each of them a hug and a kiss on the cheek.

"I love you both so much."

"We love you, too," they answered in unison.

## CHAPTER SIXTEEN

*H*al had picked her up at the airport in Tucson and it surprised her how happy she was to be back, not just to be with Hal, but to be in her second home again. It was October but to her had the feeling of early September in Maine. The sky was the deep blue that always amazed her and she sighed, relishing that she was here once more. He was going to stay with her a couple of days at first rather than driving back and forth to Tucson to give them more time to get reacquainted after having been apart for the past six weeks.

"I had Stephen pick up a few groceries to get me started," Sharon replied in response to Hal's question about whether they would need to stop on the way.

"Stephen?" he asked.

"He's the guy Joseph recommended to keep an eye on my house. He owns a company that does that sort of thing for the snowbirds," Sharon explained. "Apparently stocking the fridge and pantry is part of their services, so that seemed the easiest way to do that and it meant we could spend our time getting to know each other again rather than grocery shopping." Sharon looked over at Hal and smiled.

"Joseph?" was his only response.

"Yes, remember, he's the contractor who built my house. I'd told you about him last spring. You're not jealous, are you?" she teased.

"Of course not," he replied more forcefully than she thought the teasing called for. This was not going the way she'd imagined. "I was just trying to connect the dots since I didn't remember you mentioning the names before."

She refrained from further comment, although she didn't fully believe that he didn't remember her previous mentions of Joseph. Hal broke the silence first and his tone was more upbeat.

"So, what's your impression so far of autumn in Arizona?"

Sharon brightened at the change of topic and tone.

"It's amazing. Maybe I've been jaded by all the years in New England experiencing the change in colors of the leaves, so I no longer appreciate it the way the leaf peepers do. It is beautiful, but there's something about this that has its own beauty. Or maybe it's just that I hate cold temperatures so much that I would think this was amazing no matter what," she added.

"You could be onto something," he chuckled in response. "I confess I feel the same way."

They spent the rest of the drive to Wilmont in conversation about her flight and Hal's various work projects. Although he was semi-retired, his workload had been increasing rather than slowing down the past couple of months.

It was a different experience when they pulled into Sharon's driveway than the one she'd had 10 months ago. It still thrilled her to be here, but her life was not the same in so many ways. She sat for just a moment, taking it all in before getting out to unlock her door. There was only her carryon bag to bring in, which Hal retrieved from the trunk of his car. Stephen had aired out the house the day before she'd arrived, so it didn't have any stale smell that it might otherwise have had after having been empty for so many months. Her plants had done well in her absence, and it surprised her to see how much they had grown. The systems that had been installed to water them had worked perfectly. She checked the fridge to make sure he had stocked it as requested and found everything in order. There was even a bottle of wine chilling there with a Welcome Home tag attached which brought her a smile.

She was about to call out to Hal to ask if he would like anything to drink when she realized he was there behind her. She turned and met his lips as he bent down to kiss her. The first kiss was soft, but the second was hard and she resisted at first, but then melted into his arms as her longing for his touch overtook her. He slid his hand down her back and squeezed her bottom as she moaned softly in response to his touch.

"Let's go into the bedroom," she whispered. "My days of making love on the floor or the kitchen counter are over," smiling as she spoke, looking up into his eyes.

"You may be right about that. Not that I wouldn't be willing to try, though," he said, raising an eyebrow as though asking if she might be willing to give it a go.

"Maybe another time, but right now after that flight and having gotten up at the crack of dawn to catch it, all I can think about is how nice it will be to be next to you on my bed."

She took his hand and led the way to the bedroom.

Despite how tired she'd been, her excitement brought her sensations to full alert, and she felt Hal's touch on her breasts all the way to her toes. Her breath became ragged as he continued kissing her lips and her neck in that place that always made her shiver. She reached out to unbutton his shirt and jeans so that she could feel his skin against hers once Hal had removed her blouse and bra. She wiggled her jeans down and stepped out of them before laying down on the bed, pulling him down with her. It had been six long weeks since they'd last seen each other and they made love with a passion of long-lost lovers, recently reunited, and each fell asleep with a satisfied smile on their faces.

# CHAPTER SEVENTEEN

They spent the next couple of days at Sharon's house, settling into a new routine. Hal had arranged his work schedule so that he would not have to take time away for that. Sharon had thought about showing him the cave she'd found last spring but decided against it, wanting to keep that discovery her secret. She wasn't sure why, but it felt like that was the right thing to do.

"How would you like to go out for Mexican food this evening?" Sharon asked. "There's a great restaurant in town so we wouldn't have to go far."

"Sounds good. I haven't had Mexican for a while," Hal agreed.

When they arrived at Dos Pollos, there was already a crowd and the only table left was at the front of the restaurant.

"If it tastes as good as it smells, this might be the best Mexican food I've ever had," Hal told her as he looked over the menu. "Is there anything you would suggest?"

"It has never failed to be good whenever I've been here. I usually have one of the combination plates, but that's more to do with my not being very adventurous. The chili rellenos is my favorite."

"Do you come often?" Hal asked.

"I don't think you could say often. It's only been maybe three times if I'm remembering correctly. I usually come with Joseph."

"Joseph the builder?" Hal asked with an edge to his voice.

"He's the only Joseph I know," Sharon said with a smile, attempting to pass it off as no big deal.

Mary showed up then to fill their water glasses and ask if they would like to order.

"Sharon, you're back!"

"I just got in a couple of days ago. It's great to be here. Mary, this is my friend Hal. Hal, this is Mary."

"Nice to meet you, Hal." Mary smiled at him.

"Nice to meet you, Mary," Hal replied as he gave her that George Clooney smile that had swept Sharon off her feet all those months ago.

"Are you two ready to order, or do you need a few more minutes?"

Hal looked at Sharon questioningly as he told Mary, "We'll have the chili rellenos combination plate."

Sharon nodded in agreement.

After Mary had walked away to place their order, Hal's face once again had a look that made Sharon uneasy and an edge was in his voice as he asked, "Your *friend*?"

Sharon was taken aback but tried to make light of it. "I feel silly at my age referring to you as my boyfriend. I'm sorry, though. Maybe I should have referred to you as my partner?" she ended questioningly. "It's never come up before and we never talked about it. How would you like me to refer to you the next time?"

He didn't immediately answer as he considered the question. "That works," he finally replied and reached for her hand and gave it a squeeze.

Sharon hadn't realized she was holding her breath but let it out as she relaxed.

They didn't have to wait long for their orders, and the mood was much better than when they'd first arrived.

"That may have been the best Mexican food I've ever eaten," Hal told Mary when she brought them the check.

"Why, thank you, that's very nice of you to say. I'll take this when you're ready," she told Hal.

Sharon had been facing the back of the restaurant so saw Joseph getting up from one of the back booths and walking in their direction to leave. She smiled and waved to catch his attention, and he smiled in return and walked to their table.

"Joseph, so good to see you!"

"You, too, Sharon. When did you get back?"

"Just a couple of days ago. Do you have a minute to join us? Let me introduce you to my *partner*, Hal Jackson," she said and smiled as she looked at Hal, but he was not returning her smile.

Joseph had started to pull out the chair next to Sharon but hesitated as he, too, could see that Hal's expression was not welcoming.

"Actually, we're just leaving. Perhaps another time," he told Joseph. "Come on, Sharon, let's go." He put his credit card back in his wallet and stood with his hand out to take hers.

She hesitated for a few seconds before turning to Joseph. "I'm so sorry. I'll call later so we can catch up." She stood and took Hal's proffered hand as he nearly dragged her from the restaurant.

When they had gotten out the door, she removed her hand from his and walked to the passenger side of his car to get in, slamming the door behind her.

"I've never been so humiliated," she told Hal, not looking at him as he started the car and drove back to her house.

"What are you talking about?" he asked.

"*What am I talking about?!* Do you not realize how rude that was?"

"I wasn't rude. I told him another time. I just didn't want to spend tonight chumming up with some guy you've been flirting with while I thought we were in a relationship."

"I have not been flirting with him. I told you, we're friends. Women are allowed to have male friends."

"Is that all it was? I didn't get that impression from the way he was looking at you," Hal answered defensively.

"I think you've got it all wrong," she replied.

They continued the drive in silence and Sharon thought perhaps the discussion was over, but as soon as they got inside, Hal brought it back up again.

"I don't want you seeing him," he told Sharon.

"You what?"

"You heard me. I don't want you seeing him again. I can tell his intentions aren't what you think they are and I don't want him hanging around you when I'm not here."

"So…. what? You don't trust me either? This is unbelievable." Sharon's anger was escalating.

"I didn't say that. I said I don't want him hanging around you," he repeated in a tone which implied that should be the end of the discussion.

"No, that is exactly what you said, whether you realize it or not. You're saying I'm incapable of handling myself and that you have to be around to defend me. I'm not a child and I will say again, I get to have male friends whether or not you like it. I really don't like feeling like I'm just a possession. I thought we'd agreed that we were partners. This is not a partnership; this is an ownership and a one-way ownership at that."

"You're hysterical. Why don't you settle down and think about this? You know I'm right and you're just becoming emotional. But the bottom line is I'm not going to allow you to be running around with him while I'm in Tucson."

Sharon's jaw dropped in disbelief both from his words and that his face had become that of Broken Wing's, a nasty man who had haunted her dreams when she had been there in the winter.

"I think you need to leave… now," she told him.

"What?" he asked, as though he could not believe what she had said.

"You heard me. Pack your things and leave… now. We're done."

"Sharon…"

"I'm not going to say it again, Hal. I want you to leave."

He stormed into the bedroom and packed his things while she waited in the kitchen. He gave her a hard look before heading out the door and telling her, "When you come to your senses, call me."

"Don't expect that to happen," she told him.

She went to the door to lock it behind him and rested her head against the door, listening to make sure she heard his car drive away, and then began sobbing.

*How could I have been so stupid? I should have seen this coming. There were red flags, and I ignored them even when Mandy and Jess tried to make me see.*

She sat on the couch and pulled her legs up, resting her head on her knees, and sobbed uncontrollably. It was some time before she had cried herself out. Hal's actions and the shock of seeing Broken Wing's face instead of his had shaken her to her core. She wasn't sure she'd be able to sleep, but after turning on the house alarm system, went to bed. To her surprise, she fell asleep much more quickly than she'd expected and didn't awake until morning.

CHAPTER EIGHTEEN

On any other day, waking to find her bedroom filled with sunshine would have started the morning on a cheerful note. This morning, though, there was no solace in the warmth of the sun's rays. She dragged herself out of bed and headed to the bathroom, grimacing at the reflection in the mirror. Her eyes were puffy and red from the tears she'd shed. She took off her clothes and ran the water for a shower, hoping it would help revive her. Feeling only somewhat better, she dressed and made a pot of coffee. It was still early, but she knew Joseph would be up and she wanted to apologize even though it was not her that owed him one.

The phone rang three times, and she was about to hang up when she heard Joseph's hello on the other end.

"Joseph, it's Sharon," her voice unsteady.

"Are you okay?" he asked, the concern in his voice coming through. "You don't sound like yourself."

"I'm okay," she answered, "but I wanted to apologize for Hal's behavior last night…"

"There's no need for you to apologize," he interrupted, with the emphasis on *you*, letting her know that he was not upset with her.

"I know, but since Hal won't be around anymore, I wanted to say it anyway. I don't want there to be any ill feelings between us."

"Am I understanding what you're saying? Did you break up with him?" Joseph asked.

"Yes, I misjudged who he was," she said, her voice breaking.

"Are you okay?" he asked again.

"Not entirely, but I will be," she answered.

"This may not be the right time to be asking, but would you like to have dinner tonight? It sounds like maybe you could use some company… just as friends," he said.

"I'm not sure if I'd be very good company. Can I let you know later?"

"Of course. Just send me a text as I might not hear the phone. I'm going to be on a construction site today and it can get pretty noisy."

"Thanks, Joseph. You're a good friend and I really appreciate your being so understanding after how you were treated."

"Like I said, Sharon. I knew where it was coming from and that wasn't you."

"I'll text you later then," she said before disconnecting.

She considered her options for the day. She didn't know what to do with herself but keeping busy was better than moping around the house all day. Her walking stick that she had hung on the wall as much as a decoration as practicality caught her eye. It occurred to her that a walk would help, so she gathered her backpack, filled her water bottles and put in some snacks, applied sunscreen, and grabbed her hat, phone, and sunglasses before heading out. She hadn't planned on any particular destination and had been distracted by her thoughts, so it surprised her to see that she had arrived at the cave she'd discovered when she had been there in the winter.

After climbing the hill to the entrance, she pounded her stick on the ground several times and stepped back while she waited to see if anything came out before turning on the flashlight app on her phone and stepping inside. It was still as she'd left it and there were no signs of animals having occupied it recently. That surprised her, but it was a relief as well. She made her way to the back of the cave where she'd found the dishes and crude loom on her earlier visit. She touched them all with her fingertips, marveling at the sense of connection she felt to them. Her thoughts drifted to the young couple they had belonged to and their sad story. She had no proof that the dreams she'd had over the months she'd been here last winter of a young Native American couple were in fact, the actual people who had placed the items in this cave but in her heart, she knew it was true. Their names were Shy Dove and Running Deer and they had been forced to leave their village in order to be together. Shy Dove had been promised in marriage to the cruel Broken Wing, the same Broken Wing whose face Sharon had seen on Hal the night before. He had pursued them after their escape but Running Deer had killed him during a struggle after Broken Wing had found them. In her dreams, Shy Dove and Running Deer had not found their happily ever after and it was with sadness at that memory that Sharon sat with the things they had not taken on their journey away from the village and the families and friends they had known. She considered the possibility once again that she had been Shy Dove in that past life and that Joseph had been Running Deer. When Joseph had taken her to the airport last spring for her return to Maine, she had seen Running Deer's face instead of Joseph's when they had hugged goodbye. Had she given Hal Broken Wing's face just to make him the bad guy in her current scenario, or was it karma playing out in this lifetime? Shy Dove had not been able to have a happily ever after with Running Deer in that past life, but was she being given a second chance with Joseph in this lifetime?

*Or am I just being a silly romantic?* she asked aloud, knowing there was no one there to answer.

It was true that she and Joseph were just friends but there had been a spark there, too, which she had pushed to the background once she and Hal had met. It was also true that Hal had not seemed at all like the Broken Wing from her dreams when they had first met. If what little she knew of reincarnation was correct, part of the point of being born again was to do things differently so maybe he had made some strides but clearly there were pieces of him, the cruel ones, that were still there below the surface. Was she, were Shy Dove and Running Deer she corrected, being given a second chance at finding lasting happiness now that Hal's true self had been revealed? She considered that possibility for a while longer before heading back to her house to text Joseph to let him know she would like to have dinner. She felt lighter than she had in a long time and it occurred to her she hadn't even known that dark feeling had been there, weighing her down all this time until it was gone. *How could someone feel happy even while another part of them knew on a subconscious level that someone they were involved with was not the right person?* It wasn't an answer she was going to spend time analyzing. It was enough to know in her gut that it could be true and that sometimes in life you had to have those experiences in order to really know what you didn't want. *Or maybe what you did want,* she told herself. And right now, what she wanted was to see Joseph again.

# CHAPTER NINETEEN

Sharon texted Joseph as soon as she got back to her house and was surprised to have him respond almost immediately. They made plans for her to have dinner with him at his house at 6:30 and she signed off feeling so much better than when she had woken up in her bed that morning. The walk and introspection had made all the difference. This was the first opportunity she'd had to go through her house by herself since arriving, and she was drawn to her craft room. Seeing the gourds and supplies she'd needed for the class she'd taken made her realize how much she missed Donna's company, so gave her a call.

"Well, hello, stranger," Donna's voice greeted her.

"Hi, how are you? I've missed you!" Sharon replied.

"When will you be back? Maybe we can sign up for that gourd class again or find something new to do this snowbird season?"

"I'm back now," Sharon announced. "I got in a couple days ago, but Hal had been here. He's gone now," her voice cracking despite her best efforts to keep that from happening.

"Is everything okay?" Donna asked, the concern in her voice coming through.

"Not completely, but I will be. I broke up with Hal last night."

"Oh, no, what happened?"

"How about you come here tomorrow, and I can tell you all about it then? I'm not sure I feel up to it today."

"Sure, I can do that. I don't have anything on my schedule, but even if I did, I'd rearrange things. It sounds like you could use a shoulder to lean on. What time would be good for you?"

"How about 11? I'll plan on having something for lunch here just in case I make a fool of myself by crying, which I do not want to do in public. Nobody wants to see that," she teased.

"Sounds like a plan. Is there anything I can bring?" Donna asked.

"Just yourself. I can't wait to see you."

"The feeling's mutual," Donna agreed.

Sharon realized she would need more groceries than what she'd asked Stephen to buy to start her out, so made a list and headed to the grocery store, humming to herself. Things were looking up.

# CHAPTER TWENTY

She arrived at Joseph's house at 6:30 and took a deep breath to settle her nerves before ringing the doorbell. Joseph's smile as he opened the door assured her there was nothing to be nervous about. He gave her a quick hug before stepping aside to let her inside.

The smell of something delicious greeted her. Sharon had been to his house for dinner once before last winter and the food then had been exceptional.

"Joseph, are you sure you've been telling me the truth about not being much of a cook? If whatever I'm smelling is not a testament to an excellent cook, then I don't know what is."

He chuckled and rubbed his cheek as he answered somewhat shyly, "I can make a couple of things, but you may have reached the end of my expertise as a cook. Let's go into the kitchen, or maybe you'd like to sit outside? It's a little cool, but I can turn on the patio heater," he offered.

"Actually, that sounds wonderful," she replied. "I'll be here longer this winter but I'm still in that mode of trying to take advantage of every minute I can to enjoy the warmer weather."

"Will you be going home at all between now and then?"

"Yes, I told the girls I'll come back for Thanksgiving and Christmas, but I haven't made my reservations yet. I'd still planned on having Thanksgiving dinner at my house, so need to get back in plenty of time to buy the groceries and do as much cooking as possible ahead of time but might only stay for a week around Christmas. New Year's Eve isn't something I've celebrated the past few years, so had been thinking I might be back here for that, but that had also had something to do with Hal. Now that we're not together…"

"Maybe you could make a new tradition, with new people…" the unspoken offer hung in the air.

"Maybe I could at that," she answered, smiling in agreement.

That was the last time that Hal was brought up and they had a lovely evening catching up on how they'd spent the time since Sharon had gone back to Maine and talking about their children. Joseph had been busier than usual with his construction business and was thinking it was time to turn over more of the day-to-day management to his son, Peter. Joseph walked Sharon to her car when it was time for her to go home.

"Thank you so much for the dinner and great conversation. I had a wonderful time," Sharon told him before opening her car door.

"Me, too. I hope we can do this again soon," he said as he kissed her on the cheek. It was just a light brush of his lips, but the hint of what could come in the days ahead brought a glow to Sharon's heart.

"I hope so, too," she told him, looking into his eyes.

She arrived home and headed to bed, knowing she would sleep well that night.

# CHAPTER TWENTY-ONE

Shy Dove groaned and rolled over on her side, trying to block out the whimpering from Shadow, but realized it was futile when he put his front paws on her and began licking her face.

*"Stop! Alright, alright, I'm getting up!"*

*It had been a full cycle of the moon since Running Deer's death. The first two weeks were a blur in her memory as she had spent most of it wrapped up in their blankets, sleeping as much as she could to keep from feeling the despair that had engulfed her. Only the need to relieve herself and eat and drink the minimum required to stay alive forced her out of bed. At first Shadow had slept by her side, perhaps seeking his own solace from the loss of Running Deer, but his recent efforts to bring Shy Dove back to the land of the living had finally prevailed.*

*Once she'd accepted that she would have to go on living, she'd thought about returning to her village but knew that was not a possibility. She would not be welcome after how she and Running Deer had left, and she wasn't even sure she could find her way back in any case. Not to mention that she might have to explain what had happened to Broken Wing, and that was not something she wanted to do. It would only be her word that Running Deer had killed him in self-defense, and she couldn't risk it. Broken Wing's father was a powerful man and who was to say that he wouldn't blame her. No, there was no point in going all that way just to die at his hands.*

*"Come on," she told Shadow after her morning ritual to greet the new day, the same one she had watched her mother do every morning. "Let's check on the plants and see what's growing."*

*Shadow trotted along beside her wagging his tail, happy to have his human back again.*

*She and Running Deer had planted the seeds she'd brought with them to start their new life and they were doing well. She might not know how to hunt but she could still survive even if all she had were the beans and vegetables, especially since now they would only need to feed one.*

*She raised her face to the sky, soaking in the sun's warmth. It felt good on her skin, but the day would be a hot one. She would tend to the garden now and spend her afternoon weaving in the shade of the ramada Running Deer had set up for her. Shy Dove missed him with all of her heart, a heart so broken she'd thought it would never mend, but there must be some purpose for her to still be alive. She hoped she would discover whatever that was soon. For now, getting through each day was purpose enough.*

# CHAPTER TWENTY-TWO

*S*haron opened her eyes and felt the wonder she'd experienced last winter as she recalled her dream of Shy Dove. It was like having an old friend come back into your life after being separated with no contact in between. She wondered if having gone to the cave yesterday had sparked this or if she only had these dreams in Arizona because of the proximity. She had not had any during her time in Maine. As had been her practice before, she found the document on her laptop where she had kept an account of all her past dreams and added this latest one. She realized she'd missed Shy Dove and had wondered what had happened to her following Running Deer's death. The thought of her being so completely alone with only their dog, Shadow, to keep her company had brought her nearly to tears.

The sound of a text coming in brought her out of her reverie. She smiled as she saw it was from Joseph.

**I meant what I said about wanting to do this again. How about dinner on Saturday?**

Sharon smiled but hesitated for just a moment to consider whether she was rushing things once again, thinking about what a mistake that had been with Hal. Was she talking herself into believing this was different and that Joseph was not like Hal? *I won't know unless I get to know him better,* she told herself before replying.

**Sounds great! When? Where?**

**I'll pick you up around 6. There's a new restaurant in town I've wanted to try. It's a little dressier than Dos Pollos but I'm ok with that if you are.**

**I'm up for it. See you then.** 🙂

**Looking forward to it!**

Joseph wasn't Hal. She knew that deep down. Even so, she vowed to keep her eyes open wider this time. She was still vulnerable, and that could cloud her judgment. It was possible that trying again so soon could be a good thing, as she would be more alert to the warning signs she'd ignored with Hal.

*I sure hope so. I can't afford to get hurt again. Twice in less than a year is more than enough!*

With that resolution made, she started making preparations for Donna's arrival.

# CHAPTER TWENTY-THREE

*D*onna arrived at 11 just as planned, and it surprised Sharon at how glad she was to see her. She'd known she'd missed Donna's company and although they'd kept up by phone while she'd been gone, it was not the same as being able to be in the same room with her friend. They gave each other a big hug before heading into the kitchen.

"What can I get you to drink? I've got water, both still and bubbly, or if you'd rather have something hot, I can make us coffee or tea," Sharon offered.

"Just plain water sounds good," Donna answered as she sat at the table.

"Now, tell me all about what happened," Donna continued once Sharon joined her, after pouring each of them a glass of water.

Sharon sighed as though to prepare herself for what she was about to say.

"I feel like such an idiot. There were red flags that I should have seen. I dismissed Mandy's warnings because I thought she was just having a hard time accepting Hal because of her loyalty to Tom. When even Jess shared her concerns, I still ignored the warnings. I don't know if I was just so lonely that I didn't want to see it or if I was just so gullible that I fell for his charm." Her voice cracked, and the tears were threatening to spill over.

Donna reached across the table and covered Sharon's hand with her own. "I get it," she reassured her. "Sometimes we make excuses for unacceptable behavior and try to convince ourselves it's nothing and overlook the explanations they give and accept their apologies even when we know down deep that they're meaningless and it will happen again. It's not a matter of if, but of when. I did that for years with my ex before finally saying enough was enough, so I have been there. What happened, though?"

"We'd had a time or two in Maine when he came out at the end of the summer when his behavior had crossed the line for me but just like you said, he apologized, and I brushed it off that it really was because he was under stress for a job he was working on. Then after I got back here a couple nights ago, we'd gone out to dinner and my friend Joseph was at the restaurant. I was introducing him to Hal and had asked Joseph to sit with us for a few minutes. Hal was rude to Joseph and when we got home, he told me he didn't want me to see Joseph if he wasn't around. I'd never seen him being jealous like that, but then again, I'd never had a situation where I was introducing him to one of my male friends. I'd thought his jealousy with the girls was just part of blending families. Tom had never acted that way, but the girls were so young, and Tom and Hal were different people. I just hadn't realized how much different they were," she finished, her voice inflected with sarcasm.

Donna nodded, encouraging Sharon to go on.

"We had a big fight, and I told him to leave that same night. Thankfully, I haven't heard from him since, so haven't needed to block his number. He may have been right about Joseph, though," she confessed.

"Oh?"

"We had dinner last night, and he's invited me to dinner again on Saturday."

Donna's eyebrows raised, but Sharon could see she was not doing so in a judgmental way. This was about curiosity.

"If I'm being honest, I'd felt some attraction to Joseph when I first came out last winter. We hit it off and both being widows, we had that in common. I'd even considered it might be going in a romantic direction, but then I met Hal and that put those thoughts to rest. When Joseph took me to the airport last April, he gave me a hug as I was leaving and I admit there were sparks between us, but again… Hal…."

Donna nodded for her to go on.

"I called Joseph yesterday to apologize for Hal's behavior and let him know we'd broken up. He invited me to dinner at his house. I went. We had a great time and today he texted me to invite me to dinner on Saturday, which I accepted," she finished. "Am I rushing things, though?" she asked.

Donna thought for a moment before answering. "Maybe. But what does your intuition tell you?"

"It feels right," Sharon told her.

"Then you're not rushing things. It sounds more like you were on the right path and just took a detour with Hal. Maybe that's what you needed for you to know that this is the right path for you now."

"I had that same thought myself yesterday. Sometimes it takes the bad experiences to appreciate even more when we have the good ones."

"Great minds," Donna winked at her.

"Thanks for listening and being such a good friend," Sharon smiled at Donna. "And now, moving on, let me hear all about what you've been doing. How's that persistent neighbor of yours?"

Donna laughed, "Still persistent, and I think he's wearing me down. I haven't said yes to his date overtures yet, but I don't think that will last much longer."

"It could be a good thing!" Sharon told her.

"We'll see," was all Donna would commit to.

The heavy conversations over, they spent the rest of the afternoon together on a happier note and made plans for Sharon to come to Tucson the next week before Donna headed back in time to miss the afternoon rush hour traffic.

Her old routine had clicked in, and Sharon felt the comfort of being in her home away from home, replacing the negativity that had overtaken her after her argument and break up with Hal. She yawned and headed to bed that night, feeling the peace she'd always felt before the turmoil he'd brought into her life.

CHAPTER TWENTY-FOUR

*hadow's low growl brought Shy Dove back to the present. She had been thinking about Running Deer while weeding their garden and had fallen into the waking dream state that task often put her into.*

*She looked around but could see nothing that would have made Shadow growl.*

*"What is it Shadow? Are you playing games with me?" she teased.*

*Shadow abruptly stood up on all fours and growled again, and the fur on his back stood on end. This time Shy Dove decided to trust his instincts and return to the cave she and Running Deer had made their home.*

*"Come," she commanded in a whisper and ran in that direction, looking around as she did to see if she could see what had Shadow upset, but there was still nothing there.*

*Once they were safely in the cave, she crawled to the edge to look out over the valley. They were high enough up that it offered protection and she could see farther. There was an outcropping of rocks that had blocked her view on the ground, but which had also protected her from being seen. Now that she was in the cave, she finally saw the stranger approaching.*

*Her hand flew to her mouth to keep her gasp from alerting him to her presence and clutched Shadow's body with her other hand to keep him from running toward the stranger.*

*"Stay," she commanded, and thankfully he obeyed, although she knew he wanted nothing more than to run down to face the stranger and protect their home.*

*She watched as the young man neared the break in the rocks, knowing that if he came around the other side, he would see her garden and know that someone was living here. He was riding a horse, so must have traveled some distance. Although she and Running Deer had not been here that long, they had never seen any evidence that others were living in the area, so had felt safe that they would not be found. There must have been others closer than they had thought, though. She let out her breath as she saw him turn his horse around and head back in the direction from which he came. Something must have caught his attention, although she could not see from where she was hiding what that might have been. She did not see anyone else, so assumed he had been alone. After giving thanks for not being discovered... this time... her mind began running through what she might do if he returned.*

CHAPTER TWENTY-FIVE

$S$haron lay in bed for several minutes after waking up, running through the dream again to make sure she remembered all the details before getting up to write it down. She realized she was also running through various scenarios that Shy Dove might take if the stranger… or any other strangers… returned to find her. It had all felt so real to her that she had to remind herself it was just a dream and even if it had been real, it was long past the time when she could have been of any help. There were more immediate matters she needed to attend to, including calling Jess and Mandy to let them know about her breakup with Hal. She wasn't sure why she hadn't done it sooner, especially since… or was it because… she knew they would be happy to hear the news. It felt a bit like hearing I told you so, even if they didn't say the words. There was also the embarrassment of knowing they had been right, and she hadn't seen what they had, even at her age. Once again, the feeling of having been taken as a fool overtook her, but she quickly shook that off, knowing that it wouldn't change anything and, as she'd heard a long time ago, feeling guilt or shame is optional. It wouldn't do anything other than to make her feel bad, and that was a choice. Today she was choosing not to go there. She sent a group text to the girls asking if they'd be available that evening to talk, since they were both working now. It wasn't long before they'd both texted back and they set up a time. With that settled, Sharon was free to go about her day.

At the appointed time later that day, she was able to connect with both of them using the three-way calling feature on her phone.

"Is everybody here?" she asked. "I'm never sure if I've done this right since I don't use this feature that often."

"I'm here," Jessica replied.

"Me, too," Mandy added. "How's it going out there?"

"Good and bad, or maybe the bad is good, too," Sharon told them.

She could hear the concern in Jess's voice as she asked, "Are you okay? What happened?"

"Hal and I broke up," she announced. "It was a couple days ago, but I needed some time to process before I let you know."

"What happened?" This time it was Mandy who asked, and Sharon was relieved that it was only concern in her tone, especially since it had been Mandy who was most against Hal's presence in Sharon's life.

"We had been out having dinner when I was going to introduce him to Joseph Ramos..."

"That's the guy who was the builder of your house?" Jess interrupted.

"That's right. We'd gotten to know each other last winter, too, and he's become a good friend who has helped me out a lot to get established here," Sharon continued. "Anyway, he had been at the same restaurant and was leaving about the same time we were finishing up, but when I asked him to join us, Hal got jealous and was rude. When we got home, he told me he didn't want me seeing Joseph, and that's when I told him we were done." Sharon took a deep breath, feeling the emotions coming back again and not wanting to get weepy. "Your father never treated me like that, and I knew I would not let anyone else do that either."

"I'm so sorry, Mom," Mandy told her. "Not that you're done with Hal, I'll be honest, but that you were treated that way. Women… and anyone, for that matter… should be allowed to have friends with whomever they choose to. You did the right thing calling him on it."

"I agree," Jess put in. "I had a feeling he might be that type, though. He obviously had a problem with us although he tried to hide it."

"Why didn't you say something?" Sharon asked.

"We tried, Mom, but you didn't want to hear it."

"You're right," Sharon agreed, after thinking about it. "I tried to dismiss it as you not wanting him around because it had happened so soon after your dad's death. I think I used that as an excuse, though. There had been some red flags, but I ignored them. It's over now, but I owe you both an apology."

"Are you okay being there on your own? Are you sure don't want to come home for a while?" Mandy asked.

"I'll be fine. I called Joseph to apologize for Hal's behavior and we're still friends. In fact, we're having dinner tomorrow. And I've gotten back in touch with Donna, my friend from the gourd class. She came here for lunch and we're getting together again next week. I think it's best if I stay here and face things like an adult. I'd feel like I was running away if I came back to Maine now."

"You're having dinner with Joseph?" Mandy asked.

Sharon had hoped she could gloss over that but should have known that Mandy's training as a lawyer would have kicked in to tweak out that detail.

"Yes, as friends," she emphasized. "My eyes are open wider so no need to worry."

"I hope so, Mom," Mandy told her. "You know I just don't want you to get hurt, don't you?"

"I know. I don't want that to happen either. Joseph is a different person than Hal is, though, so I'm not worried about that happening. And like I said, friends," she said, immediately questioning herself whether that was all it was. "Enough of that for now. What have you two been up to?"

They spent the next twenty minutes catching up before ending the call. Sharon hung up, wondering if she'd been covering up once again by not saying more about Joseph. Was this just a repeat of what had happened with Hal? Why else was she so reluctant to tell the girls there might be something more? She acknowledged that maybe she was afraid to admit she felt that, both to herself and to them. She was still confused about where it was going. A part of her was caught up in the dreams and seeing Joseph's face as Running Deer's but how could she know if that was real or merely her imagination trying to fit pieces into a puzzle that didn't belong? Her instincts told her that Joseph had feelings for her that went beyond wanting to just be friends and, if she was honest, she had those feelings, too. Maybe as Donna had suggested, Hal had just been a detour. One that had led her onto a very rocky road, but that was over now, and she decided to let it go and just let it be. She could spend the rest of the day going over it in her mind but realized that analyzing it to death would not make her feel any better. She picked up her iPad and opened the Kindle app, hoping that reading a book would distract her and stop the loop playing in her head, not sure it would work. Before long, though, the magic of being lost in a good story took hold.

# CHAPTER TWENTY-SIX

Joseph showed up on Saturday wearing slacks and a button-down shirt that was a step above the usual ones he wore while on his construction sites.

"Don't you look handsome," Sharon told him after inviting him inside.

"And you look beautiful," he told her.

She'd finally decided on a skirt and blouse combination with low heels, not knowing just how dressy the restaurant would be. "Why, thank you! Let me just grab my sweater and purse and I'll be ready to go,"

They arrived at the restaurant fifteen minutes later. It was new since Sharon had left to go back to Maine the previous spring.

"From what I hear, they have a nice variety of menu options, but the specialty is steak," Joseph told her.

"I got busy working on a new gourd project and forgot to stop for lunch, so I'd eat just about anything they offered right about now," she joked.

Joseph gave the hostess his name for the reservation, and

they were seated in a quiet corner. The restaurant was already busy, which was a good sign that the food would be delicious.

"Looks like they're doing well," she commented after having made her meal choice.

"Yes, and I don't think it's totally because it's new. That sometimes happens when a new place opens up but if the food isn't worth it, then it won't last long."

"They've done a nice job of making it upscale without being snooty," Sharon said, looking around at the interior design.

"Snooty?" Joseph teased.

"Yeah, snooty. You know, pretending to be something pretentious," she smiled back at him, knowing he was teasing, not making fun of her.

"In that case, I agree. It is not snooty. So, tell me about what you've been up to since we saw each other."

"Well, my friend Donna came to see me and we're going to meet up in Tucson next week. I've done some grocery shopping, talked to the girls, worked on a new gourd project like I was telling you earlier. I can hardly keep up with my jet-set lifestyle," she said as she rolled her eyes. "How about you?"

He laughed before telling her, "I can't compete with that. My days have pretty much been get up, go to work, go to bed, wash and repeat."

"Have you thought about retiring at all?"

"I've been too busy to even consider it until now. Business is good, but it's taking its toll, too. I'm not the young man I was all those years ago and the long hours and physical work are getting to me. It's hard to admit for someone like me, but it may be time to let Peter take over more of the daily tasks. He's been good about letting me come to that decision on my own, although I know he's been thinking it."

"It's funny, isn't it? At some point, our kids become the ones who are giving us the expert advice. My girls tried to warn me about Hal, but I couldn't hear it. I thought since I was the grown up, they were misjudging him. Turns out they were right after all, and the roles had been reversed."

"Have you heard from him?"

"Thankfully, no. I don't think I will, and I've got his number blocked on my phone to make sure that doesn't happen."

"Probably a good idea," Joseph agreed. "I know I shouldn't say this, but I'm glad he's out of the picture. This may be too soon, but I'd hoped last winter we could get to know each other better. I'm not sure where it's coming from, but I feel a connection with you, Sharon."

She could see the sincerity in his eyes but had told herself she wanted to take things slowly.

"I feel a connection, too, but…" she hesitated. "I want to make sure I'm not jumping into this. I made a big mistake with Hal and even though I don't think you're like him, I want to be certain. It's about trusting my own feelings again. Maybe it's a good thing. I think it's my way of acknowledging that you are special, and I don't want to mess it up."

"I can wait. I've waited a long time already," he said.

Sharon shivered, thinking about her dreams of Shy Dove and Running Deer. Joseph's words held a deeper meaning for her than he could ever know.

Joseph turned down her offer to come in when he brought her home. Even though it was Saturday, he let her know that he would have to be on a job site early, so needed to get his rest. He gave her a kiss on the cheek before leaving and she let herself in, calling it an early night herself. It wasn't long after getting in bed with her iPad to read that she felt sleep overcoming her and shut the cover, rolled over and fell immediately to sleep.

# CHAPTER TWENTY-SEVEN

*It had been two weeks since the stranger had nearly discovered her without making another appearance. During that time, Shy Dove had taken out Running Deer's bow and arrows to examine how they had been made to see if she could remake them to fit her. She had tried to use them, but the size was too big to overcome for her tiny frame. Her experience with weaving had given her the skills needed to see how things fit together and she had watched Running Deer make arrows, so with some time she had been able to fashion the bow and the arrows he had left into a usable size. Her aim was still off, but she had practiced every day and was getting better. Even if no one ever approached her space again, which she knew was unlikely, she would be able to hunt small animals now to add to the vegetables in her garden. Shadow had fed himself by hunting nearby, but he never left her side for long.*

*She was weaving under the ramada, facing the direction the stranger had approached, when Shadow padded up to her with a rabbit in his mouth. He dropped it at her feet and looked up at her as if to say, I've brought you something.*

*"Shadow, are you sharing your rabbit with me?" she asked,*

*surprised but pleased. It would be a nice treat to have fresh rabbit after living on the dried meat she still had stored.*

*Shadow gave a short bark in reply as Shy Dove laughed. As she bent to pick it up, though, he began to growl and lowered his head. She thought she had misinterpreted his intentions until she could see that he was not looking at her, but beyond her. She sensed that there was something behind them and slowly reached down to bring the bow and arrows in front of her so that she could notch an arrow in the bow, hoping that she had not given herself away.*

*"Quiet," she whispered to Shadow, as she could see that he was about to bark. She wanted to know what they were dealing with and whether it would be better to run or try to scare away whatever was there.*

*Shy Dove shifted from her sitting position to kneel on her haunches and slowly turned around, bringing the bow with her. She gasped as she could see a young man staring at her from atop his horse about 50 yards away. Jumping up, she planted her feet and let the arrow loose, but her aim was off, and it fell short of its intended target. She grabbed another arrow and ran toward the cave as fast as she could, hoping she might be able to hide before he could catch her, but realized there was no way she would be able to outpace the horse and stopped.*

*"Go away!" she shouted at him as he dismounted his horse.*

*He had not seen Shadow racing toward them, but the horse nickered and strained against the reins in the stranger's hand, distracting him.*

*"Shadow, here!" Shy Dove called, and the dog ran to her side, although she could tell that he wanted to attack the stranger instead. She notched the arrow in her bow and pointed it at the young man who looked to be about Running Deer's age. "Go away!" she shouted at him.*

*"Are you here alone?" he asked, still holding onto his horse, who had calmed but was looking at Shadow with a wary eye. He*

*was as tall as Running Deer and she could see he was muscular beneath his clothing. She could tell that it would be unlikely that she could fight him off.*

*"My husband is here, just around the other side of the rocks. He will be here any moment."*

*"I don't believe you," the stranger replied. "If he was that close, he would have either already been by your side or he would have killed me by now."*

*"He may be smarter than you give him credit for." She purposely looked past the stranger to trick him into thinking there was someone behind him, but he did not turn around as she'd hoped.*

*"I still do not believe you," he replied, but did not approach any closer. "Why don't you put down the bow and tell me why you are here by yourself? I promise I won't hurt you," he told her and raised his hands to reassure her he was sincere. "Besides, I don't think I would even have time to reach you before your dog would attack me. Here, I'll sit down to prove to you that I won't attack while you tell me your story," dropping to the ground and crossing his legs in front of him.*

*Shadow continued to growl as Shy Dove debated whether to give in. She realized she had little choice. Even if she could turn and run, there was nowhere to hide, and she didn't want to give away the location of her cave. She also realized that she was lonely and having someone to talk to, even someone she did not know or trust yet, was proving to be too strong an urge to overcome. Slowly, she lowered the bow and sat on the ground herself as Shadow sat down beside her. She stroked the fur on his head to let him know it was okay.*

*"How do you know my tongue?" she asked.*

*"I trade with the people to the south and have learned your language. I recognized it as soon as you told me to go away," he smiled.*

*"Oh," she replied, considering this, and worrying that he*

might have heard about a missing young woman and man. Or possibly even about Broken Wing, whose body they had left to the elements after he had attacked Running Deer and they had struggled to the death.

The stranger waited patiently for Shy Dove to go on.

"What is your name" she asked him, "and where is your village?"

"My name is Horse Spirit, and my village is beyond those hills, about a two-day ride from here. What is your name?"

She thought about whether she should tell him her real name. If he had been to her village, he may have heard her story and want to take her back.

"My name is Cactus Blossom," she told him after spotting a prickly pear in bloom.

"What is your husband's name?" he asked.

"His name is Deer Hunter. I lied when I said he is here now, but he will be back soon. He is out hunting," she added. She wanted him to believe that she was not alone except for Shadow.

"How long have you been here? And why are you alone?"

"We came here about six moons ago, but why we came is none of your business," she answered with her chin lifted, defying him to contradict her.

"That could explain why I've never seen either of you before. I've only recently started coming in this direction or I'm sure I would have found you before this."

"Will you leave us alone now?" she asked, hoping that he would not betray her presence to anyone else. "We wish to be on our own and we can provide for ourselves."

He looked at her for several minutes, judging whether to pursue his questioning and deciding to let it go... for now. He knew she was not being completely truthful with him but did not want to push her too far. Now that he knew she was here, he could come back again on the pretense of offering goods for trade.

*"As you wish," he smiled and rose to his feet again.*

*Shadow jumped up and began to growl, but Shy Dove patted his head to let him know she was in no danger. She hoped that was true and their conversation had given her some sense of feeling that she would be safe. She followed him at a distance as he turned his horse around and walked toward the ramada on his way out of her land.*

*"Your weaving is exceptional. Would you be interested in trading?" he asked.*

*Shy Dove realized the wisdom of doing so if she was going to stay here. She had not yet found the resources to keep up with her weaving once the supply of materials she'd brought with her was gone and there might be other goods she would need in the future.*

*"Perhaps," she answered, "but not today. I will need to discuss this with my husband," she added, to continue the ruse that she was not alone.*

*"Of course," he smiled in return. "I will be back here in another moon cycle and will stop on my way. That should give you and your husband time to decide. And perhaps there would be other things you might need as well."*

*"Thank you. I will let him know of your offer and that he should expect you then."*

*He mounted his horse, gave her one last appraising glance and rode away.*

*Shy Dove bent down to hug Shadow to her, ruffling his fur.*

*"What do you think, Shadow? Can we trust him?"*

*Shadow whined and licked her face as though to tell her he was not sure.*

# CHAPTER TWENTY-EIGHT

"It's so good to see you again," Donna exclaimed, pulling Sharon into a hug when she arrived at Donna's condo the next week.

"You, too," Sharon agreed.

"How are you doing with the breakup?"

"I think I'm mostly over it now, other than still feeling a bit embarrassed that I ever got into it in the first place," Sharon admitted.

"You weren't the first and you won't be the last, but as long as you've learned from your experience… notice I'm not saying mistake… then it's not such a bad thing," Donna told her.

"You're absolutely right, and I think I have. I've had dinner a couple of times with Joseph, but we're taking it very slow and building up the friendship before we take the next step. We were already good friends, so it's not that much of a leap, but I have a better feeling that I'm not rushing in this time."

"I hope so, honey. I hated seeing you hurt like that," Donna told her as she reached out to stroke her arm. "Come on, let's go out on the balcony and enjoy the sunshine."

They walked through the living room area of Donna's

condo out to the balcony that overlooked the pool. There was no one there at this time of the day during the week and the snowbird season was still in its early stages. Sharon relaxed in the comfort of being with a good friend with whom she could share her feelings and be an objective observer to give her advice. She had never been one to have a lot of friends, preferring the solitude, and she'd always had Tom's company in the past. It wasn't that she shunned social interaction and could be social when the occasion called for it, but she wasn't the type to reach out to others to seek it. Having one good friend was enough, and Donna fit that perfectly. They had quickly formed a bond last year, and she hoped they could get to be even better friends this winter now that she would be in Arizona even longer.

"What do you think we should try this winter?" Donna was asking her.

"Have you ever thought about weaving?" Sharon asked. Her dreams of Shy Dove had piqued her interest in the skill.

"Weaving? I can't say that it's been something I've ever thought of trying, but I'd be up for giving it a shot. Should we check out Groupon to see if there are any classes on sale coming up?"

"I hadn't thought about doing that, but sure," Sharon agreed.

They spent the next half hour researching possible class options and finally found one that looked like it would work. The shop where it was held not only had the supplies but also had looms they could rent so that they would not have to buy the equipment. It was also during the day which Sharon appreciated so that she would not have to make the drive in the evening. It began the next week and would run through the middle of December, which would also work out well, although Sharon would miss at least one class while she was back in Maine for the holidays.

"Would you be up for going to the shop now to check it out?

We could grab some lunch while we're in the area. I seem to remember a good sandwich shop nearby," Donna suggested.

"Sounds good," Sharon agreed.

They found the shop and, after signing up for the class and picking out the supplies they would need for the project, decided to go to lunch at the sandwich shop Donna had mentioned. Sharon stopped dead in her tracks and Donna nearly bumped into her.

"What's wrong?" she asked, confused.

"That's Hal at the table in the corner," she answered, her voice shaking.

Donna looked over in the direction Sharon had indicated.

"The one with the guy canoodling with the hot blonde who looks about twenty years younger than he is?"

"Yes. Can we just get out of here?" she asked, trying to turn around to leave before he would see her, but Donna was right there. Just then, Hal looked up and spotted her. His face showed only a brief expression of surprise before smiling at her and then leaning down to whisper something in the blonde's ear. The blonde giggled and kissed him on the lips as Hal held her face in his hands.

"Come on, let's go," Donna took Sharon's arm and left the restaurant.

Sharon held it together until she got into the car, and they were driving away before the tears started.

"How could I have been so naïve?" she sniffled. Before Donna could answer, though, her anger overtook her. "What a jerk!" she exclaimed. "I've been beating myself up about how I handled our breakup, but now I'm actually glad I saw that. If I wasn't over him before, I definitely am now!"

Donna glanced over at her to see if she was okay.

"In that case, I'm glad you did, too," she told her. "Do you still want to get some lunch?"

Sharon considered whether she would feel like eating and

decided that would be best. She wasn't going to give Hal even one more second of renting the space in her head.

"I do, and I'm sorry if I made that uncomfortable for you," she apologized.

"You're not the one who owes anyone an apology," Donna reassured her. "I just wanted to make sure you were okay. Being upset has the effect on me of eating even more, but I know that's not how everyone rolls."

"Thanks. You're a good friend. You know that, right?" she smiled at Donna.

Donna smiled back. "So are you, girlfriend. So are you."

They found another restaurant not far away and after a good meal and conversation, Sharon was in a much better mood as she headed back home later that afternoon.

# CHAPTER TWENTY-NINE

*S*hy Dove had settled into a routine of tending to the garden in the morning and weaving in the afternoon. She'd also continued to practice with her bow and was getting much better. Shadow still brought her a rabbit to share every few days. She'd almost forgotten about Horse Spirit's promise to stop when he came through on another trading trip. Shadow's growl alerted her to his presence, but not in time for her to hide in her cave.

"Cactus Blossom, I was hoping to see you," he called out. "Have you spoken with your husband about trading your blankets? Is he here?" he asked, looking around and dismounting from his horse.

At first Shy Dove was confused until she remembered that she had told Horse Spirit her name was Cactus Blossom.

"My husband is nearby. We have not made a decision about the weaving, though," she replied. "Perhaps you can try again when you are on your way back from your trading mission."

"I can wait awhile until he returns. He won't be long, will he?"

Shy Dove felt trapped. She still didn't know if she could trust

*Horse Spirit, and it could be dangerous for her to admit that she was alone.*

*"I don't know how long he will be. He was going to hunt and will be back as soon as he can find something for our evening meal. It shouldn't take long but I wouldn't want to keep you from your journey, and you may pass him along the way," she said hoping he would leave so that she would not have to keep up the pretense and have him catch her in her lie.*

*"I do not mean to make you afraid. I promise you I will not harm you," Horse Spirit said in a gentle tone. He held out his hand for Shadow to sniff, hoping to befriend him.*

*Shadow's growling had stopped, but he had remained by Shy Dove's side. He looked up at Shy Dove to ask permission to sniff Horse Spirit's outstretched hand. At her nod, he sniffed cautiously and then gave Horse Spirit's hand a tentative lick.*

*"He is well-trained. I'm glad you have him with you to keep you safe while your husband is away."*

*"Yes, my husband trained him from the time he was a puppy. He has been a good companion for me," she said and realized that might have given away that she was alone. She did not see any recognition in Horse Spirit's expression that he had caught her slip, but he was looking down at Shadow and she may have missed it.*

*"I should get back to my weaving. Thank you for stopping and perhaps I will have an answer for you upon your return."*

*She hoped he would take the hint that she wanted him to leave as the more time that passed, the more obvious it would be that Running Deer, or Deer Hunter as she'd told Horse Spirit, would not be coming back.*

*He looked into her face and then gave Shadow one more scratch under his chin before standing up to leave. She kept her expression blank and satisfied that there was no point staying longer, he turned to walk back to where his horse was waiting patiently and effortlessly climbed on its back.*

*"Goodbye, Cactus Blossom. I'll be sure to come back. I look forward to seeing you again, whether you decide to trade your blankets or not. Perhaps there will be some other way I can help you," he said, smiling and waved his goodbye before turning his horse and heading toward the south.*

*Shy Dove breathed out in relief. She would need to come up with some other excuse upon his return, but she knew she could not keep the lie up forever. It had bought her some time, though, to figure out what would be the best way to deal with this. She did not want to have to leave what had become her home. It was lonely with Running Deer gone, but an acceptance that this was her life now had come over her once her initial grief and passed. They had found a beautiful location with a stream that provided water, the cave for shelter, and the land was providing food. What more would she need? As a sense of loneliness came upon her with Horse Spirit's departure, she acknowledged she might be missing another human to interact with more than she had realized.*

# CHAPTER THIRTY

They arrived early for their class and found places near the front of the room, then looked through the handouts that had been left on the table. They'd chosen the Navajo weaving class since it would be more portable, and they could take their projects home to work on them. It was not being taught by a Navajo, but according to the handout, the instructor had lived for many years on a reservation as an elementary school level teacher and had at first been self-taught. She recounted a story of having been told by the weavers in the community that she could not possibly learn to weave the Navajo way, but once she showed them her work, they agreed to include her and she continued to improve her skills. It was a small class that had been limited to only six students and as the time for the class to begin approached, the remaining four students, all female but a range of ages and ethnicities, showed up. The class began with everyone introducing themselves and telling why they'd joined the class. The group, as often is the case with creative types, was welcoming and encouraging each other to do well.

After giving them a brief introduction of herself and her experience with weaving and then going through the handouts, the instructor began the class with teaching them all how to warp their looms.

Sharon had listened attentively to the instructor, but at first the warping was confusing. As she settled herself and let her fingers take over, she felt a sense of serenity overtake her. It was as though she'd reclaimed a piece of herself that she didn't know had existed.

"You're a natural at this," the instructor told her. "Have you woven before?"

"Oh, thank you," Sharon said, broken from her concentration. "No, I never have but I've always wanted to learn so was very excited to find your class."

"I hope you enjoy it and if you have any questions, let me know," she said before turning to Donna, who was not having as much success.

"I think I see what's tripping you up," the instructor told her and explained the process again after taking out the places where Donna had gone wrong.

"Yes! Now that makes a lot more sense. Thank you," Donna told her and seemed to relax as she started over again, but on the right track this time.

"So much easier when you're doing it the right way," she told Sharon.

Sharon chuckled.

"How did you catch on so quickly?" Donna asked her.

"I don't know. It just seemed to come to me like I'd done it before, even though I've never woven anything more than those potholders I think we all may have done when we were kids," she said.

Sharon debated telling Donna about the dreams she'd had of Shy Dove. They'd never had conversations about their beliefs in spiritual matters of any kind, much less reincarnation. Maybe that was the way to broach the topic before she brought up the dreams. It didn't seem like Donna would be the type to put her down for her beliefs, but still, there are some things you don't bring up in casual conversation. She'd had enough experience over the years with those who looked askance at anyone who didn't follow the conventions of traditional religious beliefs, at least as far as those practiced by most Americans and scoffed at anything that sniffed of what they dismissed as New Age nonsense. Telling Donna about the dreams was one thing since everyone had dreams, but to admit that she believed they were memories of a past life experience was quite another. She decided to hold off at least until she knew if Donna was accepting of that possibility, or until she felt comfortable enough sharing it even if she wasn't, but that it wouldn't interfere with their friendship. She valued that more than the need to share the dreams.

It seemed like the class had barely begun when the instructor told them it was time to wrap things up. They'd all managed to get their looms warped and chatted excitedly about the next week's lesson when the fun would begin, and they could learn the weaving techniques. The project that they would all be doing was a stylized design that would incorporate several techniques and give them an overview so that they could continue on their own after the class ended.

"Well, what do you think?" Sharon asked Donna as they walked out to her car with their looms.

"It took me a while to get the hang of it, but once Shari showed me the second time, it finally clicked. I really think this is going to be fun and I've always admired the Navajo weaving style, so having my own small wall hanging will be something special. Great suggestion!"

They had come together, so had a little more time to chat as Donna drove back to her condo where Sharon had left her car.

"What do you think about reincarnation?" Sharon asked tentatively.

Donna glanced over at her.

"Where did that come from?" she asked but Sharon didn't get the vibe that Donna was put off by her question.

"Just curious. We've never really talked about that sort of thing, but I was thinking about it while I was warping my loom. There was something very familiar about the process and it made me think about some people believing that skills that come naturally are because the person had done them in another lifetime. I wondered what your take on that was."

"Well, I don't know that I could say I definitively believe it and I'm more in the camp of there's so many things in this life we don't understand so try to keep an open mind to the possibility it could be true," Donna told her.

"That's where I am, too. Have you ever had anything happen that might make you think you've had a past life experience?"

"You mean like meeting someone you immediately connect with and feel like you've known them all your life or going someplace that feels familiar even though you've never been there before?"

"Yes, exactly!"

"No, never had that happen," Donna said in a serious tone and then they both burst out laughing.

"Yeah, actually I have and you're one of those people," Donna confided. "Do you think we might have been friends in another lifetime?"

Sharon didn't need to think long before replying, "Yeah, I had that immediate connection to you at our first gourd class. I just knew that we would hit it off, which is why I struck up the conversation. I'm not usually one to reach out to people like that."

She considered whether to go on and decided this was the perfect segue into telling Donna about her dreams.

"You asked me in class about how I caught on so quickly and I sort of brushed it off. That's what really had me thinking about the reincarnation angle. Ever since I came out here last winter,

I've been having these dreams of a young Native American couple. I'm not usually one who can remember my dreams, but these have been so vivid and real that it's like I'm watching a movie, so I've been keeping a log as soon as I wake up after having one. The young girl and her mother were weavers."

"Is that why you were interested in taking the weaving class?"

"Yes, actually. It's really piqued my interest and I guess on a subconscious level I wanted to see if I had that ability, too, possibly as validation that it was possible."

"Huh," Donna replied, "if this class was any indication and if there really is such a thing as reincarnation, you may be onto something." She looked over at Sharon and smiled, reassuring her it would be okay to discuss this topic in their future conversations.

"If you're willing to share, I'd love to hear about the rest of the dreams you've had. You said they've been happening for a while now?"

"Yes, and each time it's like another episode of a television series because they've come to me chronologically following their life."

"Very cool," Donna said.

"If you're really interested, maybe I can print off the document that I've been keeping and let you read it," she offered.

"Really? I'd love to read it!"

"It's a deal then," Sharon said, and hoped she wouldn't regret the offer. The dreams had been so special, she hoped sharing them wouldn't diminish them for her. Or worse, jinx herself and she wouldn't have any more dreams. She had a feeling Shy Dove still had a lot to tell her and she wouldn't want to miss any of it.

# CHAPTER THIRTY-ONE

It had become Sharon and Joseph's routine to text each day and at least once a week they would get together for lunch or dinner, and their friendship had continued to grow. It wasn't the pace that had been the hallmark of her relationship with Hal, and Sharon was more than okay with that. Her encounter with him at the restaurant had once and for all put that to rest for her. What she had with Joseph felt right, and the doubt that she'd ignored about Hal was absent. They had kept the relationship platonic so far, not that there wasn't a spark for either of them, but they had agreed that they could wait until they knew this was going to take the next step into a committed relationship. It came as a bit of a surprise to Sharon, then, when Joseph invited her to join him for dinner along with his children the week before she was to return to Maine for the Thanksgiving holiday.

"I've told them I'm dating, and they asked to meet you," Joseph told her when he brought it up.

"Oh, of course. I don't know why I'm surprised but…" she trailed off.

"It feels like meeting the parents?" he asked, teasing.

"Yeah, I guess that's exactly it," she smiled.

"I promise it's no pressure. I've told them we are just friends for now but you're the first woman I've dated since Susan passed and they're not sure what to make of it."

"I get that. I felt like I was a teenager again and that the roles were reversed when I let the girls know I was dating Hal. In his case, they were right to be concerned."

"You have nothing to worry about and definitely don't need to compare yourself to him," he said, and she could tell that he still had negative feelings about his brief encounter with Hal.

"I confess this makes me nervous, but sure, I'd love to meet them," she said, hoping it would be a more enjoyable reception than Mandy had given Hal when they'd first met.

Joseph gave her the day and time for the dinner and refused her offer to bring anything other than herself.

When the day arrived, Sharon found herself becoming more and more nervous. She didn't want to make a poor impression as she didn't want anything to complicate the future relationship with Joseph. She knew what a strain it had put on her relationship both with Hal and her girls. The last thing she wanted was to put Joseph in that position. She took extra care in picking out her outfit to portray an image of a woman who was not a gold-digger or too flashy, not that there was much of anything in her wardrobe that would have conveyed either of that. Discarding the first three options, she settled on a pair of black slacks and a white button up blouse with a turquoise cardigan that brought out the blue in her eyes and silver hair. She never wore much jewelry in any case but limited it to a pair of plain silver small hoops and her watch and kept her makeup to a minimum. Nothing more than a sheer foundation, mascara, and light pink lipstick.

"You can do this," she told herself as she locked her door behind her and got in the car to head to Joseph's house. There were already two cars in the driveway when she arrived, signaling that his children were there.

Joseph's smile and reassuring hug as he answered the door and welcomed her inside put her more at ease, but she took a deep breath to calm herself as she stepped into the foyer. She could hear conversation and children's laughter coming from the patio, which gave her a chance to repeat her mantra in her head "I can do this" as Joseph led the way.

"Everyone, I'd like you to meet my friend, Sharon Peterson. Sharon, this is my son Peter, my daughter Melinda and her husband, David, and those two monsters are my grandchildren, Joey and Maya."

"*Papa!* We're not monsters," Maya told him, putting her hands on her hips, making everyone laugh.

"My apologies. Sharon, these are my grandchildren, not my favorite monsters," Joseph said seriously, but with a twinkle in his eye, the love he had for them shining through.

"I'm so delighted to meet you all," Sharon said, looking at each of them in turn. "Joseph has told me so much about you, all good, of course." She realized how lame that was, exactly what every stereotypical greeting would be. She told herself she wasn't making any great first impressions, but the smiles she received in response felt genuine, so it might not be as bad as she feared.

"Dad reminded me we'd built your house out on Silver Spring Road, the one with all the eco sustainability features," Peter said.

"Yes, that's right. That's how we met. Your company did a wonderful job. It was one of the best experiences I've ever had with having a house built and it's a joy to live in," Sharon warmed to the subject. "Your dad has been a big help since I've been here doing my snowbird thing and we've become good friends," she added.

"I think it's been good for Dad, too," Melinda smiled at her father with warmth and not a hint of disapproval in her voice.

"You're right about that," Joseph agreed. "It's nice to have someone my age of the opposite gender to spend my time with. There's only so much of construction site talk a person can handle and I'd gotten into a rut. I didn't even realize how much I needed another friend until I met Sharon."

She could feel her cheeks getting pink and was glad she hadn't put on any blush, or it would have been even more noticeable but despite that, also felt like the evening would be less stressful than she'd feared and that being accepted by Joseph's family would not be something she needed to worry about.

"I'm sorry, we've had you standing here all this time," Joseph said as the introductions had come to an end. "Come on in and have a seat and let me get you a drink. What can I get you?"

"Water would be great," she told him. She'd thought about having a beer, but she was a lightweight when it came to her tolerance for alcohol, and she didn't want to take any chances of embarrassing herself.

Joseph brought her a glass with a slice of lemon, just as she liked it, and sat next to her on the couch with his arm resting on the back of the cushion above her shoulders. He wasn't touching her at all, but she felt his presence, reassuring her she was one of them.

Sharon left later that evening before the others feeling accepted and encouraged that this was a good sign for her and Joseph. At least that hurdle of meeting the family had been crossed, and perhaps when she was back in Maine, it was time to tell Jess and Mandy that she was dating again. She'd resisted doing so before this in case it didn't look like things were going to work out, especially so soon after she'd broken things off with Hal. She didn't want to hear any rebukes from the girls about jumping into another relationship, although Mandy would probably be the only one to do so even though Jessica might be thinking it. It wouldn't be easy by any means, but her gut told her it was going to be easier this time. She didn't know why, but she was going to trust her instincts and hope for the best. She'd find out soon enough.

# CHAPTER THIRTY-TWO

*Shadow's growl alerted Shy Dove to the sound of horse's hooves approaching. She looked up and could see a man on a horse with another horse laden with bundles following behind in the distance and grabbed her bow and arrows that she kept beside her at all times after Horse Spirit's first appearance. She hid herself behind an outcropping of rocks, telling Shadow to stay with her and brushed his fur as much for her comfort as his. As the rider and horses got closer, she could see that it was Horse Spirit. She hadn't expected it to be him because she had only seen him with one horse in the past. It made sense that he would need the second horse to carry the goods he must have traded for since he'd last been through.*

*"Cactus Blossom, are you here?" he called out.*

*She debated staying where she was until he left, but her need for human interaction won out and she came out from behind the rocks with Shadow trotting beside her to greet him.*

*"Horse Spirit, welcome," she told him. "You've arrived once again when my husband cannot meet with you, but we have discussed trading my blankets and he has told me he is agreeable to making a trade."*

"I'm pleased to hear that," Horse Spirit said, dismounting from his horse. "I must have very bad luck to always arrive when your husband is away, though. I would very much like to meet him. Is there a better time for me to come?"

Shy Dove had been practicing different scenarios to tell Horse Spirit, knowing that this would come up.

"I cannot tell you when, but he has said that you and I could bargain without his approval. The blankets are mine and the only goods we would need would be ones I would use," she said, trying to convey a tone of authority and hoping he would believe her reason for Running Deer not being involved.

"I see," Horse Spirit answered. He had his suspicions about this being true but decided not to push her. Her weaving was of excellent quality and would bring him a high price for other goods. He also thought that if he could continue to befriend her, the truth would eventually come out. He was curious why this woman was here, seemingly alone and far away from her tribe based on the language she spoke, but thriving nonetheless, and he was patient. A trait traders needed to be successful, and he was very good at what he did.

"Well, then," he continued. "How many blankets are you willing to trade and what would you like to trade for them?"

Shy Dove hesitated for a moment, not sure if she wanted to go to the cave to bring them down as it would reveal where she lived when she was not at her garden or ramada. She realized she would have to do so, though, and at some point she would either have to trust Horse Spirit or move, and she was not prepared to do that. Setting aside that it would be too much to do that on her own, she did not want to leave this spot where she had made her home, as it would also mean leaving Running Deer. Yes, he was dead, but his spirit was still here with her and she could visit the grave where she had buried him as she did every day since he'd died, telling him her thoughts and how much she missed him and loved him still.

*"Stay here and I will bring them. Do you have any pots for storage? My beans will ripen soon, and I will need more pots for those and the corn once that is ready."*

*"I do. I can get them while you go for the blankets. Perhaps we could do that under the ramada to stay cool," he suggested.*

*"That is a good idea," she agreed, thinking that might also give her time to bring the blankets back without being seen. She realized, though, that even though the cave was not that far away, it would take her time to climb the hill and bring them back. Shy Dove was still going to have to trust Horse Spirit as there was no way she could avoid his knowing where she stayed when she was not in the cave. She felt some relief that he had stayed at the ramada as he'd suggested when she came back with two blankets. It was all she'd had time and materials to make.*

*"These are beautiful," he told her. "You use designs that are traditional, but you do them in such a way that makes them unique. I've only seen something similar once before in a village far to the south of us."*

*Shy Dove held her breath, afraid he would tell her he knew her secret, but when she did not respond, he changed topics.*

*"These are the pots I have. I would be willing to trade all of these for one of your blankets. Is there anything else you need?"*

*They both knew he was being generous with the trade, but Shy Dove needed more materials for weaving and so asked if he had any.*

*"I do. Let me get that."*

*He brought back both cotton and wool, some that had been dyed and some that had not. Her eyes lit up, seeing the raw material and thinking of what she could do. He noticed her excitement and knew that under other circumstances he could have taken advantage of that, but it was not how he wanted to proceed. Patience would pay off in the end.*

*"Would you trade me all of this for my other blanket?" she asked.*

*He did not respond immediately, even though he planned to do that for her. He had to at least act the part of a barterer so he would not arouse her suspicions as to his motives.*

*"I can do that this time," he answered. "You drive a hard bargain."*

*Shy Dove's expression told him he may have gone too far.*

*"The real reason I am being so generous is that I want to make sure you will have more blankets for me to trade," he admitted.*

*Shy Dove nodded as this was a more believable explanation, as even she knew he had been too eager to agree to her request.*

*"In that case, I accept your offer and you may have my other blanket in exchange for all of this."*

*Horse Spirit smiled and Shy Dove relaxed, as she could sense his sincerity, and she felt he would be someone she could trust. She had watched Broken Wing's father, Eagle Feather, trade in her village, and although his mouth had smiled, his eyes rarely did. She didn't think she would ever have trusted him to not take advantage of her had she been trading with him.*

*Pleased with how this had turned out, she offered Horse Spirit to join her for her midday meal, not sure if he would accept. He hesitated at first, thinking about making more distance toward his village, but he'd had a long ride already and his horses could use a rest. He also wanted to see if he could get Shy Dove to open up about where her husband really was, if there even was a husband, that is.*

*"Thank you. If you're sure your husband would not mind."*

*Shy Dove realized her mistake as soon as he mentioned her husband, but there was no way to back out now.*

*"I'm sure Deer Hunter would want me to be gracious to you after you have been so kind," she said. "Perhaps he will be back*

*before we are done so that you can finally meet him," she added, hoping it would convince him she was telling the truth.*

*"I hope so. I would very much like to meet him," Horse Spirit said.*

*"I'll be right back. Stay here, Shadow." Shy Dove told him and left to get the supplies she needed to make them corn cakes, taking as many of the pots with her as she could carry.*

*"Let me help you with the rest of this," Horse Spirit offered.*

*"NO," Shy Dove said more forcefully than she intended. "No," she repeated, smiling as she did so. "You are my guest, and I can finish this later. I just thought since I was going there anyway that I would take some of this away."*

*"Of course," Horse Spirit said, but he suspected the real reason for her hesitation was that she did not want him to see that there was no evidence of anyone else living with her. He'd kept his face blank when she'd told him that Deer Hunter might be back soon. It was his skill as a trader to know when someone was hiding something and clearly, she was still trying to hide this. Now that he'd earned some trust, he didn't want to push her. He knew she would be here the next time he came through, as she had not left by now. He watched as she left but made no move to follow, in part knowing that Shadow would try to stop him if he did, but also knowing he could just be patient.*

*Shy Dove returned soon and began making the corn cakes for them, glancing at Horse Spirit, who had taken his horses to the stream to water them.*

*"What do you think, Shadow? Should we trust him?" she said in a low voice.*

*Shadow whined and licked her hand. She decided that was a good sign.*

*Horse Spirit left the horses at the stream, knowing they would not leave without him, and walked back to the ramada.*

*"They smell wonderful. I didn't realize how hungry I was. It's been several days since I've had any food cooked for me."*

*She smiled back at him and passed him a bowl of food and water to drink. They ate for several minutes without more conversation before Horse Spirit spoke.*

*"How long have you been here?" he asked.*

*"Only a few moon cycles," she replied, hoping he would not continue his questions or asking why they were here.*

*He sensed her discomfort and switched tactics.*

*"You picked an excellent location."*

*"Yes, it's perfect," she agreed. "We knew as soon as we saw it that it would have everything we would need."*

*He could tell that she would not say more, even though he remained quiet. Sometimes that would encourage others to continue to say more than they would have otherwise just to fill the silence. He decided to finish his meal and continue on his way to his village. He still had not mentioned finding her to anyone there and would not this time, either.*

*"Thank you for your food and your company. I should go now, but I will stop again soon. Please tell your husband you did well," he said.*

*She stood to walk with him to his horses and waved as he rode away.*

# CHAPTER THIRTY-THREE

It was another late-night arrival and had a very different feel from when she'd come home in the spring. There wasn't the anticipation of having someone new to share her home, which had turned out to be a good thing. Still, it felt odd to be in another location, even though this had been her home for most of her life. How could she be homesick for a place where she'd spent such a short time living, but that's how she felt about being away from her winter home in Arizona and was glad that this time she'd only be away for a couple of weeks. The one thing that was the same was having to tell her children that there was a man in her life. The friendship with Joseph was still platonic, which might make a difference. Sharon knew she was the adult, and it was her life to live, but she didn't want this to be another drama. She'd already arranged for the girls to come for dinner the following evening and would let them know then.

The next day went by quickly, doing errands that mostly involved grocery shopping in preparation for Thanksgiving. She'd given herself enough time to buy a frozen turkey that would be thawed by Thanksgiving day, and it was a small one, so there wouldn't be a lot of leftovers since she would be flying back to Arizona the following Sunday.

Jessica arrived first and Mandy followed shortly after, both seeming to be in good spirits, for which Sharon gave a silent prayer of thanks.

"How was your flight?" Mandy asked.

"Not bad. The flight connections went off without a hitch, so that's my idea of a good flight," Sharon said. "Can I get either of you something to drink?"

"Coffee if you've got it," Mandy said.

"Coffee's good for me, too," Jessica said.

They gathered at the kitchen table and Sharon decided to dive right in with her announcement.

"I need to tell you something and thought it best to do so right up front. You know that I broke up with Hal and that's definitely over," she emphasized as she could see by their expressions that they were ready to step in to voice their objections if she was still involved with him. They both seemed to relax but were still on alert, knowing that there was more.

"I've been dating Joseph Ramos, the contractor who built my house. It's still a platonic relationship and we're taking our time to get to know each other. I didn't rush in this time like I did with Hal, so think I learned my lesson there. It may not be more than friendship, but I have a feeling it will, and it feels different for me. He's a very different person than Hal, for one thing. He invited me to meet his children and grandchildren last week and I'm hoping you'll be willing to meet him when you come to visit in February, assuming we're still dating, of course."

Jess and Mandy exchanged glances to see who would speak first.

"I really don't know what to say, Mom," Jessica finally spoke. "You know all I want is for you to be happy and it sounds like you are, but that's how you felt about Hal, too."

"Exactly," Mandy interrupted. "Just be careful, Mom, okay?

It sounds like you are trying to do things differently this time and you are an adult. You have your own life, as you've told us before," she said, smiling, so Sharon knew she had taken that declaration from their previous discussions to heart. "I will do my best to keep an open mind and let you figure this out for yourself."

"Thank you," Sharon said.

"But…" Mandy said, "if my spidey senses tell me he's a loser, like they did with Hal, I'm going to let you know."

"Same for me," Jess added.

"That's all I can ask," Sharon told them.

With that out of the way, they could move on to catch up with the more mundane topics, such as meal planning for Thanksgiving.

Sharon thought it might have been a mistake to wait so long to come back, but she hadn't wanted to miss another weaving class and had convinced herself she'd be able to get everything ready for the holiday if she remained organized. That was mostly true, but it was an exhausted Sharon who boarded the plane back to Tucson on Sunday. They'd had a wonderful holiday dinner together, which included the girls' boyfriends. She'd sent them all home with full stomachs and enough leftovers so that she wouldn't have to waste anything when she cleaned her refrigerator before her trip back. Since she was going to be gone for such a short time, she'd driven to the airport herself and parked in the long-term parking area. Her drive back to Wilmont seemed longer than usual, but she reasoned that was because she was so eager to be back, and it might have been a mistake to take the later flight as it was now dark, and she was tired from the flight and time zone change. Depositing her carryon in her bedroom, she debated the pros and cons of making herself stay awake, but her fatigue won that battle and she crawled into bed, knowing it was likely she would be awake long before the light of dawn cast its first rays.

# CHAPTER THIRTY-FOUR

*he sky was a deep blue with no clouds to break its expanse and the day had quickly grown hot. Shy Dove had woken early to do her gardening chores before moving to the ramada to work on her latest weaving project. The materials she had received in her trade with Horse Spirit had given her an idea that had taken over her imagination, and the magic of weaving had cast its spell with her. She had spent her every spare minute working on it and it was nearly done. She stretched her arms overhead, hearing a soft pop as her spine realigned itself and she came back to the present as though awakening from a dream. Shadow lay beside her, his paws twitching, and she smiled, knowing that he was dreaming, too. She looked around to bring herself even more into her surroundings when she saw movement at the entrance to her cave. She stiffened and shook Shadow to waken him with one hand and grabbed her bow and arrow with the other. A man was coming out of the cave and looked in her direction, their eyes meeting. It was Horse Spirit. She remained where she was as he headed down the hill on the trail that her footsteps had worn into the dirt, her mind whirling with thoughts of how she would explain the obvious signs that she was the only one living in the cave. There would be no escaping explaining why Running Deer was not here. If he asked, that is. She would not volunteer that information, though.*

*"Greetings, Cactus Blossom," he called out as he approached.*

*Shadow had jumped up but remained with Shy Dove. He no longer growled at Horse Spirit, but he did not run toward him either, knowing that his place was by her side, guarding her.*

*"Greetings, Horse Spirit. I did not hear you coming until I saw you at my home. Where are your horses?"*

*"They are on the other side of the rocks. I didn't see you here and thought you might be in your home out of the sun."*

*She knew that had to be a lie as there was no way he would not have been able to see her, but she did not challenge him, in words at least. She met his eyes and did not look away, letting him know she did not believe him.*

*He quickly changed the subject as he saw her weaving. The colors she had dyed the yarns he'd brought were unlike any he'd seen before, as was the design. In addition to the usual geometric patterns typical of other blankets, she had woven the shapes of birds in flight above a mountain range. This was a painting in cloth, unique to anything he had ever seen before.*

*"Cactus Blossom, this is amazing. Where did you learn to do this?"*

*"It just came to me. I saw it in my head, and it took me many attempts, but then it came to me how to do it and my fingers took over for what was in my mind."*

*He looked at her with admiration.*

*"I was not mistaken to make that bargain with you for the materials. I knew your blankets were unique, but I had no idea just how talented you are."*

*She was suddenly shy and all she could reply was, "Thank you."*

*"Is this a blanket you will be willing to trade?" he asked, trying not to show his eagerness and failing.*

*"I... I don't know," she hesitated. "I'd thought so, but it's so beautiful. I'm not sure if I want to give it up. I know I could make myself another, but I think I would rather make another to sell instead and keep this one. I could also use it as a pattern if I kept it," she said, as much trying to justify it for herself as for Horse Spirit.*

*He wasn't able to hide his disappointment but did not argue with her.*

*"Do you have enough materials to make another? If not, I can bring you more," he offered.*

*"I should have enough to make one this same size, but then they will be gone. It will take me some time to do that, though, so I would not have one ready for you to trade for another moon cycle."*

*"I can wait," Horse Spirit assured her. "There will not be any others like this... except for yours, of course," he smiled, acknowledging that she would keep this one.*

*She smiled in return, happy with the bargain they'd struck.*

*He frowned in thought before bringing up the topic she'd been afraid he would. He looked into her eyes, seeing the fear there.*

*"Cactus Blossom, I will never hurt you," he told her, and she believed his words. "You know that I was in your cave."*

*She only nodded in agreement.*

*"I can see that you are the only one who is here. You do not have a husband, do you?"*

*She did not look away, but she did not respond immediately. At last, though, she knew she could no longer avoid telling him the truth.*

*"My husband is here. I am not alone...."*

*Horse Spirit looked as though he was going to dispute her words, but she rushed on.*

"…. he is here, buried beside the rocks there." She nodded her head in the direction of the outcropping near the trail that led to her cave. "We came here together, but he was killed by a mountain lion not long after we arrived. I've been taking care of myself, with Shadow's help, since then." She ruffled his fur as she spoke the words and her chin raised, daring Horse Spirit to dispute her ability to fend for herself.

"I hope you will not betray me to anyone," she went on. "So far you are the only one who has found me."

"That has only been a matter of luck," Horse Spirit told her. "My village is two days from here by horse, but that will not keep others from coming this way before long. What will you do then?"

Her fear was beginning to overtake her, but she fought it to put on a brave face. "I've been practicing with my bow and am getting better. I can protect myself. Would those from your village wish me harm or would they be friendly as you have been?" she asked.

"I think they would not hurt you, but they would want to know why you are here," he said.

"I can't tell you that," she replied. "It's too…" her voice trailed off, fearing she may have already said too much. It was still a possibility that he might have heard the story of their escape and try to return her to her village.

"When you are ready to tell me, I would like to hear your story, but I will not force you to do that today," he said.

She let out a deep breath, thankful that he would not pursue this for now.

"Is there anything I can do for you?" he asked gently.

"No, I'm fine," she replied, perhaps more harshly than she'd intended. "Shadow and I have managed on our own and we are doing okay, aren't we, Shadow?" she scratched the top of his head. He barked once in agreement.

"Yes, you are," Horse Spirit smiled as he agreed with them.

*"I will be on my way now, but before I go, is there anything you need until I am next here?"*

*"Just your promise that you will let no one know we are here," she told him.*

*"I promise," he told her, and she knew she could trust his word.*

# CHAPTER THIRTY-FIVE

It was a lazy day, which was a blessing, as Sharon's energy was in the negative column. Her body's ability to bounce back after the cross-country flights and dealing with jet lag wasn't what it had once been. She almost regretted having come back between Thanksgiving and Christmas but knew that in another day she'd be feeling better. Her excitement about the weaving class tomorrow helped to compensate for the grogginess she was feeling now. She put on a sweater before heading out to the patio, as the day was still cool. The bright sunshine helped, and she raised her face up to the sun to soak it in. Her phone's ring tone brought her back, and she smiled as she saw Joseph's name on her screen.

"Good morning," she greeted him.

"Good morning to you, too. Did you have a good trip?" he asked.

"It was. A bit more hectic than I'd thought it might be getting everything together, but I'm glad I made the trip. Thanksgiving is my favorite holiday, and I would have missed being with the girls."

"We would have loved to have you with us," he told her.

"Maybe next year you could invite the girls to come here for Thanksgiving."

"I might just do that. We're planning for them to come out in February, and I told them I'd like them to meet you. I hope that wasn't out of line."

"Of course not. I'm looking forward to it," he said. "Does this mean we're going steady?" he teased.

She laughed before responding, "I don't know. Would you like to be?"

"I think I would," he replied, but serious this time.

She wasn't sure how to respond. A part of her wanted to tell him she wanted that, too, but the other part of her was cautioning restraint after her experience with Hal.

"Too soon?" he asked.

"Maybe. I really like you, Joseph, and even before I met Hal, I was feeling a closeness to you. After being swept off my feet by him, I dismissed it and now I'm afraid I might be rushing into another relationship too soon. My guard is still up, I guess."

"That's completely understandable. I can be patient."

"Thank you. If it's any help, I don't think you'll need to be patient for long."

* * *

THEY HAD dinner at Sharon's house that evening. She'd kept it simple, steaks on the grill, vegetable kebobs and a tossed salad. It was going to be a cool evening, but the patio heater enabled them to eat their meal outside and enjoy the stars.

"I admit it surprised me that Mandy didn't make a big stink," she was telling Joseph as they were drinking a glass of wine after finishing their dinner. "I'm hoping that's a good sign, either that she's more willing to admit I'm an adult who can make my own life decisions or that she is a better judge of character than I was even though she hasn't met you."

"I'd say let's go with the latter," he winked at her, "but after thinking about that again, it might actually be saying that you aren't a good judge more than it's saying that my character is worthy."

She chuckled. "Good save. You're not just a pretty face," she teased back.

He laughed out loud. "I have to say that's the first time I've ever been told that."

She just smiled in return.

"Are you still planning to go back for Christmas?"

"I am. In a way, I wish I'd stayed in Maine to avoid having to do the flight one more time, but I didn't want to miss any of the weaving lessons."

"You're taking weaving lessons?" Joseph asked.

"It's this year's adventure with Donna," Sharon answered. "We found a class on Navajo weaving and signed up when I first came back this fall. I'm really enjoying it so far."

"Good for you. I bet you're good at it."

"I've always thought I'd enjoy weaving but never tried before. This class was easier to get into since we didn't have to buy a loom," Sharon told him.

"Good thinking. It's always more fun to have someone learning along with you, too," Joseph said.

"Yes. Donna thinks I'm a natural, but she's doing well with it, too. She's just not giving herself enough credit. It does feel like it's familiar to me, though. Some of the techniques are complicated at first, but the instructor does a good job of explaining them."

"When you're ready to show me, I'd like to see your project," Joseph said.

"It's a deal. It should be finished by the time this session is finished if I keep at it during the week. We're able to bring the looms home with us to work on them," she explained. "I think I'd like to sign up for the next session that starts in January. It will give me something to do during the winter. Enough about me, though, how about you, is work still as busy?"

"It is. We picked up another project and still have three other houses we're working on. Peter has done a fantastic job with sales and hiring good crews. I'm thinking it may be time to let him take over more responsibilities."

"Is that hard for you to do?" Sharon asked.

"A little, but mostly because I don't know what I'd do with my time than because I don't think he's capable," Joseph said.

"That can be a tough transition, especially for those who devoted most of their lives to their work and didn't leave time for hobbies or other interests," Sharon agreed.

"I had always wanted to travel more," he told her. "When the kids were growing up, we really didn't have the money. By the time they were on their own and I could do more of that, Susan got sick and then after she passed, working filled the void she left."

"How about now?" Sharon asked.

"It's a conversation I plan to have with Peter soon. I want to make sure he's ready before leaving, especially with things picking up. I'd like to have more free time, though, so maybe we could at least start transitioning to a part-time arrangement."

"That sounds like an excellent compromise," Sharon told him. "Traveling is something I've always wanted to do more of, too. Maybe we could try that together."

"You're a woman after my own heart," he smiled at her, taking her hand in his.

She smiled at him in return. Twining her fingers in his, she felt the warmth and solidity of his hand, roughened from his labors, and a sense of peace overtook her. They sat there together in silence, enjoying the wine, the stars and, most of all, each other's company.

"As much as I would like to stay, I really should be going. It's a busy day tomorrow," he told her as he stood up and pulled her up with him. He put his glass on the coffee table before taking hers and doing the same, then pulled her close to him. He kissed her lightly on the lips once and, as he felt her response, kissed her again deeply.

Sharon's response was immediate. She'd been holding back with physical affection, wanting to be sure this time that what she was feeling was not just lust. Her body was ahead of her mind, though, and apparently hadn't gotten the memo. She raised her hands behind his neck and the touch of his body next to hers, feeling his warmth and his scent, slightly spicy and altogether masculine, was making her breath come faster. He broke the embrace, much to her dismay, and kissed the top of her head.

"I should head home," he told her, his voice soft. "I want to stay but I want you to be sure."

She took a deep breath to regain her composure.

"You're right. I don't want you to be, but you are," she smiled up at him.

He kissed her again and took her hand to walk back into the house, grabbing the wine glasses along the way. They said their goodbyes and made plans to see each other again soon. She closed the door softly behind him and headed to bed.

# CHAPTER THIRTY-SIX

*It had been less than the cycle of the moon that she'd thought it would take, but Shy Dove had finished the second weaving and would have it ready for Horse Spirit when he returned. There was a part of her that couldn't wait for that to happen. She was eager to show him the weaving, which had turned out even better than the first now that she'd had more practice creating pictures as well as geometric shapes. She realized she also craved human companionship and hadn't known how much she'd missed it after Running Deer's death until Horse Spirit had showed up. Tending to the garden, practicing shooting with the bow, and weaving could only fill so many hours and as much companionship as Shadow was, he could not talk. Now that Horse Spirit knew she was alone but had not threatened to harm her or take her away from her home, she could relax more when he was around. Even as she had that thought, she heard hooves approaching, and Shadow was on alert. She changed her line of vision so that she could see who was approaching, but they could not see her. No one else had been this close to her cave other than Horse Spirit, but he'd warned her that others might find her, and she didn't want to take any chances of being seen. To her relief, it was Horse Spirit and his second horse that he used to carry the goods he traded who were coming her way. She moved out from behind the rocks so that he would see she was there and waved her hand.*

*He waved back and urged his horse to go faster. She could see that his horse was carrying large sacks of goods, so it must have been a successful trading trip for him. She hoped that he would have more weaving materials, as she had used every bit of what she had on hand for the second blanket.*

*Horse Spirit smiled at her as he dismounted his horse and told her, "I'll be right back. I want to give them some water," and led them to the stream. He took the packs off as well, which could only mean that he had something for her and that he intended to be staying for longer than a hello.*

*She went to her cave to get the blanket and then waited with Shadow for him to return to the ramada. She could tell from his expression that he was even more impressed with her blanket than he had been after seeing her first attempt.*

*"I think it came out even better," she said with pride in her voice.*

*"You are not mistaken. I have no words for it. I know I shouldn't be showing you how much I like it as that's giving away my hand for bartering with you but, I can't help myself. It is amazing, Cactus Blossom."*

*She thought briefly of telling him that her name was really Shy Dove but decided not to. If he had heard the story of her escape with Running Deer, he would be looking for someone with the name Shy Dove, not Cactus Blossom. It also struck her that a new name would be fitting. She had begun a new life for herself, and she was no longer the Shy Dove that had left her village all those months ago. Perhaps it was time to think of herself as being Cactus Blossom, not just for Horse Spirit's benefit.*

*"Were you able to bring me more weaving materials?" she asked. "I used everything I had to finish this one."*

*He smiled in acknowledgement. "Yes, I did. I hope you'll like what I have and there may be other goods that you might need... or want... as well. This blanket is worth much more than a simple trade of more weaving materials."*

*She frowned in thought of what more she might want, as she already had all she needed to survive. There surely had to be something she could ask for, but nothing came to mind.*

*Horse Spirit could see that she was having trouble coming up with something to ask for, so suggested coming with him to the horses where he'd left all his goods. "Perhaps when you see what I have, there may be something you will want," he told her.*

*"Yes, that might be helpful. Sometimes you don't know what you want or need until you see it," she said, smiling.*

*He unpacked the weaving materials first so that she could see what he'd brought her. Her thoughts began spinning, seeing in her mind all the blankets she could make. He had also brought some food and spices that she had been missing after she'd run out of the supplies that she and Running Deer had brought with them. She could, of course, still eat the food she prepared, but the extra flavor that they gave the food not only made it more enjoyable, but it reminded her of home and her mother's cooking. She'd thought that would be all she would ask for when she spotted a piece of green stone among some beads and other colored stones and feathers.*

*"Do you like this?" he asked, picking up the piece of rock. "I found it in a cave south of here near a village where I sometimes trade. It looked like it had been used at one time but abandoned and someone had built a wall to hide where they had stored some of their possessions. There was a pile of these rocks there as well. Cactus Blossom, are you alright?" he asked.*

*The color had drained from her face as she realized it could have been, and probably was, the cave that she and Running*

*Deer had used to hide their supplies while they were planning their escape. The same one where he had first taken her to show her the green stones—malachite—that Horse Spirit now had. She had a piece in the bag she kept with other prized possessions that had meaning only to her. Before replying, she took the piece of rock and held it in her hand, feeling the rough edges and examining it from every side. This was what she wanted. She already had the other piece, but for whatever the reason, she wanted.... no, needed.... this one as well. It was a piece of her home and she felt that there must be a message why it was being shown to her now. She didn't know what it was, but she knew its meaning would come to her.*

*"Cactus Blossom?" he asked again.*

*"Yes, I'm sorry. I would like to have this, too," was all the explanation she gave him.*

*He had a feeling there was more to her reaction but did not press her.*

*"Of course. Are you sure that is all you would like... the weaving materials, the spices, and the rock?"*

*"Can I have all of them for just the one blanket?" she asked, hoping he would say yes, but not daring to believe her one blanket was worth all of that.*

*"You should ask for more," he told her.*

*"No, this is all I need, and you were so kind with the last trade of materials, that I feel I still owe you."*

*"As you wish. Let me help you carry them to your cave," he said.*

*She hesitated for a moment, but since he'd already been in the cave and knew that she was alone, she saw no reason now not to allow him to help.*

*"Thank you, that would be helpful," she said.*

*They gathered the items up in a basket that Horse Spirit had among his other items, and Shy Dove considered asking him for that as well. It would be useful to store her weaving supplies in.*

*He saw her looking at it but decided to wait until they were in the cave to offer it to her as well. It would make it less likely that she would refuse to keep it if it was already in place. It had straps that went around each arm, making it easier to carry like a backpack, and he easily hoisted it onto his back for the trip to the cave.*

*She had taken extra care making the cave not only comfortable but beautiful as well. She had made small colorful rugs that she'd put on the floor for sitting and under her pots, which also protected the clay from becoming chipped or otherwise damaged. Her belongings were neatly stored, and she'd brought in sage that she'd tied up and hung on the wall, which gave the cave a pleasant smell. Horse Spirit immediately felt a sense of serenity upon entering the cave.*

*"You have made a welcoming home here, Cactus Blossom."*

*The praise warmed her, but she also felt the sense of loneliness that had become more acute since he'd been visiting her. She hoped he would stay longer and offered him food and water.*

*"I would be honored," he told her. "It's been a long ride and I could use a rest and I think the horses would appreciate it, too. I'm also hungry and have been thinking about your corn cakes since the last time. You add something that I have never tasted before. It's not just your weaving that is special."*

*She returned his smile and told him, "That will be my secret. That will give you a reason to visit me again."*

*"I won't need an excuse," he told her. "I would come even if it wasn't for the blankets you weave or the corn cakes."*

*Shy Dove could see in his eyes that his words were true but also that she could feel safe being alone with him. She knew some men used women for their own desires, not caring if the woman wanted their attention, but Horse Spirit did not give her the feeling he would be one of them. She would keep her guard up, but her trust was growing.*

*The cave was cool, and the day was getting hot, so she made* the corn cakes in the space Running Deer had made for them to cook and brought out some cooked rabbit she had not been able to finish from the night before. They ate the meal while Horse Spirit told her more about his trading trip and the places he'd visited.

It had been mid-afternoon when he arrived and now the day was turning to night. They had been enjoying each other's company and had not realized how much time had gone by.

"I should go before it gets too dark," he told her.

"You could stay here tonight," she offered shyly. "Perhaps your horses would do better with more rest, and you could be on your way in the morning instead."

He thought for a moment before replying, "Are you sure you would be okay with that?"

"You could sleep at the ramada so you could be near the horses," she said.

He seemed to be disappointed about that idea but didn't want to have her feel uncomfortable either. This was a compromise he could live with. He felt the sense of wanting to protect her within him and knew that his feelings for her were growing beyond mere friendship. Was she perhaps feeling the same? He wanted to find out.

"I will stay tonight then and leave tomorrow," he said.

Shy Dove felt a slight twinge of guilt at how happy that made her, but a part of her also knew that Running Deer would not have wanted her to spend the rest of her life alone. He would always have a piece of her heart, but there was room in her heart for more.

# CHAPTER THIRTY-SEVEN

The phone's ring tone brought Sharon back into the present. She'd been intent on her weaving and felt a kinship to Shy Dove, understanding how she must have felt when she was wrapped up in its magic.

"Scott, this is a surprise," she said.

"I hope I didn't catch you at a bad time."

"No, I was just weaving, but it's not something I can't stop for now and might be a good idea, anyway. I forget how long I've been doing it and then my back reminds me later."

"In that case, I'm glad I called. I have something important to ask and although it's a little old-fashioned, I want to do this right," he said.

Sharon had a feeling she knew what was coming but that he would do this even in this age and time, gave her a new respect for him. She waited for him to go on.

"I think you know how much Jess means to me and you know I will always love her and treat her the way she deserves," he said.

"I do," Sharon said.

"Then, I hope you will give me your blessing to ask her to marry me."

"Of course! When do you plan to ask her?"

"I want to give her the ring at Christmas. You are still coming back, aren't you? I know she would want you to be part of this."

"I was planning to be there anyway, but I wouldn't miss this for the world!" Sharon told him. "I have no doubt she's going to say yes, but you don't have to worry about me spilling the beans before then either," she reassured him.

"I trust you. It's me I'm worried about. I have the ring already and it will be a test of willpower for me to wait, but I want you to be here to be a part of it, too."

"Thank you, Scott. That really means a lot to me. And welcome to our family,"

"Thanks, Sharon."

She sat there after they'd disconnected, thinking about all the changes that had happened in the past year. She wouldn't be surprised if Michael and Mandy soon followed with wedding plans. Maybe they'd make it a double wedding, but if she knew her girls as well as she thought she did, they'd each want their own celebration and who could blame them. There was even more reason now to be returning to Maine and her excitement about the trip overtook the dread of another plane trip back and forth. Her reservation had been made to leave after the weaving class was over and she'd have at least two weeks there, so not everything would have to be done in a rush. But now there would be even more to do as she wanted to make extra sure that the Christmas get-together would be special. She was bursting with the excitement but had promised not to say anything to Jessica. She could tell Donna, though, as there was no worry that she'd be ruining the surprise.

"I have the most exciting news," she told Donna as soon as she answered the phone.

"What's up?"

"Jessica's boyfriend just called to ask for my permission to marry her. He wants to pop the question at Christmas when I'm back for the holidays."

"That was really sweet that he asked. I didn't realize guys still did that these days."

"Well, I don't know if they all do but it was really sweet. I was very touched that he would ask me. I know Tom would have been pleased, too. "

"Do you know if she'll say yes?"

"I would be extremely surprised if she didn't, and I can't think of any reason why she would say no. They've been going out for a few years now and I had a feeling this was heading in that direction when I was home for the summer, which she confirmed, so it didn't come as a complete surprise to me when Scott called."

"It sounds like you're going to have an exciting Christmas," Donna said.

"Now I can't wait to go home," Sharon replied.

"You'll be finishing up the weaving class first, right?"

"I will. The timing turned out perfectly with the class. It was very considerate of them to work that around my schedule," she pretended to claim.

"Wasn't it, though?" Donna played along and they both laughed.

"How's your project coming?" Sharon asked.

"Not bad, although when I look at yours compared to mine, I think I should have taken remedial weaving. I'm still up for taking another session in January if you think you'd like to continue, though."

There was no hesitation as Sharon replied, "Yes, I really do want to continue. I enjoyed the gourd class, but the weaving has felt like it's a part of me."

"Maybe you were a weaver in a past lifetime," Donna teased.

"You know, I think you may be right," Sharon answered, thinking Donna may have been more right than she knew.

# CHAPTER THIRTY-EIGHT

"I'm going to miss you," Joseph told her the night before she was to return to Maine a couple of weeks later.

"I'll miss you, too," she told him, and the words were more than just a rote reply. They'd continued to take things slowly and although they'd briefly discussed what their future together would be, had agreed to put the more serious discussion on the back burner until she returned.

"Do you think you'll stay longer now that you'll probably have a wedding to be planning?"

"I'm not planning to for the moment but leaving my options open. My guess is that there's no need for me to be there now and these days the distance isn't as big a factor to planning as it would have been. A lot of it is done on the internet in the early stages anyway, I would think. I also don't want to be the Momzilla of this wedding."

"Momzilla?" he asked with a frown on his face.

"You know, the mom who tries to take over all the planning and generally makes a nuisance of herself. Jessica is a grown woman, and this is her celebration. I'll be there to support her and help in any way I can, but I'll be following her lead, not the one leading the charge."

"Smart woman," he said.

"Thank you," she told him, smiling.

"How do you think Mandy will take the news?"

"They're actually really close and although Mandy can be competitive and a bit bossy, I think she'll be happy for Jessica. At least I hope that's how it will play out. I won't be around to act as referee, and I'd be disappointed if she tried to be a drama queen."

"Time will tell. In the meantime, I have a little something for you. I left it in the truck, but I'll be right back," he said. He came back with a small gift box that looked like a jewelry size box which he handed to Sharon.

She unwrapped it and her mouth dropped, and goosebumps raised on her arms when she opened the box. Inside was a necklace with a delicate silver chain and a wire-wrapped polished green stone that she immediately recognized as malachite. They had never spoken about Sharon's knowledge of malachite before and the significance of Joseph giving her a necklace with that specific stone did not escape her.

"It's beautiful," she told him with awe in her voice.

"I'm so glad you like it," he told her. "I just had a feeling when I saw it that you would."

"You have no idea how much," she told him and kissed him gently on the lips.

# CHAPTER THIRTY-NINE

She'd already bought most of the gifts she planned to exchange with the girls and Scott and Michael in Arizona, so could focus on decorating instead. It would not be on the scale that she'd done in the past as she wouldn't have as much time following the holidays to take everything down before her trip back, but she wanted the house to have a festive spirit especially knowing that this year they would have even more to celebrate. They'd made plans to get together on Christmas Eve, knowing that the girls would also be going to their respective boyfriends' extended family gatherings on Christmas Day. She did another walk through the house, inspecting what she'd done so far, and was pleased with how it had turned out. She had to admit that there was something about celebrating Christmas with the chill in the air and snow on the ground. There had been no snow when she first arrived, but the weather had cooperated in the spirit of the season, and she'd woken up to a winter wonderland. It was only a couple inches of snow, which was hardly enough to consider a snowstorm for them but was just enough to make it feel like Christmas for someone who had spent most of their life in New England. The grocery shopping had been done the day before, so she could concentrate on the cooking today.

Scott and Jessica arrived first with their arms full of packages and what looked like a bottle of champagne. Scott gave her a wink as he handed it to Sharon in the kitchen while Jess put the packages under the tree.

"Is this the night?" Sharon asked him, whispering so Jess wouldn't hear.

"I hope so. I have the ring and my speech all memorized. Do you think it's still a good idea to ask her in front of everyone?" he asked, needing her reassurance to calm his nerves.

"It will be fine," she told him, giving him a squeeze on his arm. "Here, take this into the living room so she won't get suspicious about why we're taking so long," she said, handing him a plate of hors d'oeuvres, following him with a pitcher of eggnog.

There was a knock at the door and Mandy and Michael came in, also carrying brightly wrapped presents and a bottle of wine. They joined everyone in the living room after hanging their coats in the hall closet and gave everyone a hug.

After a few minutes of everyone chatting, Scott cleared his throat and tapped his glass with a fork to get their attention. Everyone looked expectantly at him, wondering what this could be about. He took Jessica's hand in his and although he did not kneel on one knee, her expression told everyone that she could see this was leading to a proposal.

"Jess, you've made my life so much richer. You are the most loving, understanding person I know, and you've put up with my little quirks better than anyone, even my parents," at which everyone laughed.

He took a deep breath and went on. "I think you know what I'm about to say, but I've been practicing this for a few weeks now, so I hope I don't mess it up. I've already asked your mom for her blessing, but now I need yours. It would make me the happiest man alive if you would agree to marry me," and he reached into his pocket to bring out the jewelry box which he opened and said, "Jessica Peterson, will you marry me?"

She could only bob her head in agreement as she was overcome with emotion and wrapped her arms around his neck before kissing him on the lips.

Everyone clapped, and Sharon wiped away the tears from her eyes. She looked over at Mandy to see that she was doing the same and she knew that there would be no jealousy or drama to deal with.

Scott took the ring out of the box and started to put it on Jess's finger before pulling it back. She looked at him in surprise but then realized he was teasing her as he said, "You haven't actually said yes yet," with a smile on his face.

"Yes! Yes, I'll marry you," she said.

He finished putting the ring on her finger and gave her a big kiss and hug.

The rest of the evening was filled with love and happiness, and everyone left in a jovial mood. Sharon closed the door behind them as they left and headed to bed, mostly happy for this next chapter in all their lives. She felt a moment of sadness that Tom was not with them to share in this part of Jessica's life but knew in her heart that his spirit was there.

# CHAPTER FORTY

The time in Maine had gone by quickly, but Sharon was glad to be returning to Arizona. She missed Joseph and although they had chatted on the phone, it was not the same as being there in person. They had made plans for him to come to dinner the day after she was back to give her a chance to settle back into the Arizona time zone.

She surprised both of them when she opened the door upon his arrival and kissed him and hugged him tight.

"I've missed you," she said.

"Really? I hardly noticed you were gone," he teased.

She punched him lightly on the shoulder and pretended to push him back out the door, but he only laughed and took her in his arms again and kissed her soundly on the lips.

"No way you're making me leave," he told her. "I've been dreaming about this moment ever since you left."

"I didn't realize just how much I would miss you," she said. "It was great to be back with the girls, but only half of me was there. I kept thinking about how much I wished we could have spent Christmas together."

He took her hand and walked her to the living room couch, where they sat next to each other.

"I think this has turned into something I want to become committed to. I've always been a monogamous man and I think you have those same values, but are you comfortable committing to that now, too?"

"I am," she said.

"That's great news. I have felt this way for a while now, but I wanted to give you the space to get over Hal and know for sure that's what you want, too."

"I so appreciate you," she told him, putting her hand on his face. "You remind me of Tom, but you're your own person, too. I'm not just trying to replace him with you, and I think I may have fallen for Hal so fast because I didn't realize just how lonely I'd been after Tom died. I'd thought I'd gotten over him, but clearly there was something going on under the surface. I'm just glad that Hal's true nature came out before I made an even bigger mistake."

"He rubbed me the wrong way from the moment you first told me about him," Joseph growled.

"I could tell."

"I don't know what it was about him, but I had the feeling that I should be protecting you from him. It came over me out of nowhere. You know how with some people you just instantly don't like them?"

"Mmm hmm. I have met several people who affected me that way. Some people want to say it's because they've had run-ins in a past life," she said, curious what his reaction might be to that idea.

"That would go in the anything's possible but not sure if I can cotton to it category for me," he said.

She decided not to pursue that topic for now. And maybe never. It didn't change her beliefs and as long as he would not disparage them, she was okay with it. She wasn't one who thought that a partner had to be in synch with every thought of the other's. It made life more interesting that way, too.

"Tell me about the wedding plans. Have they set a date yet?"

"They're thinking June, and it will be a small wedding. Neither of them are the flashy kind and they want to pay for everything themselves, so will have a budget. I plan to go home in the middle of May as there will be last-minute things to do and I want to help as much as I can. I want to stay here as long as possible, though."

"This is probably selfish, but I'm glad to hear that you won't be going back sooner."

"If it is, then that makes two of us who are selfish."

# CHAPTER FORTY-ONE

*orse Spirit had slept outside with the horses. The way he'd looked at her told her he would have liked to stay with her instead. Shy Dove had been unsure if she should invite him to sleep in the cave with her, but perhaps it was for the best that he hadn't. She was still confused about her feelings for him and being disloyal to Running Deer's memory. From her vantage point in her cave, she could see Horse Spirit packing up his things so called to Shadow to come with her to say goodbye.*

*"Good morning, Horse Spirit."*

*"Good morning, Cactus Blossom. Did you sleep well?" he asked.*

*"I did. And you?"*

*"It was a beautiful night, and this spot is a peaceful one. I think I slept better last night than I have for a very long time."*

*"You're welcome to sleep here anytime," she said before thinking through what she was about to say, and her face turned red.*

*He smiled a big smile and gave her a look that made her tingle inside.*

*"I would like that very much," he said.*

*She could not find any words to respond.*

*"I have embarrassed you. I'm sorry," he said, putting his hand on her shoulder.*

*"It is alright. I must have meant it but...." she hesitated to find the exact words she wanted to say. "I loved my husband with all my heart, and I was afraid I was dishonoring his memory." She looked in Horse Spirit's eyes to see if she could see understanding there.*

*"I do not think you would be dishonoring him. You have shown nothing but honor for his memory since we first met. You are a woman here alone, and yet you made a point of making me think he was still with you. I can tell that even now you did not want to take advantage of this situation. I promise you, Cactus Blossom, that I will do nothing to dishonor his memory either, but you are a young woman who has much of life left to live. I do not think he would want you to be alone. Would it be so bad for you to have a friend?"*

*"I think you are right. Running Deer always wanted me to be happy."*

*"Running Deer?" he asked, and Shy Dove knew she had slipped. She had told Horse Spirit that his name was Deer Hunter. "Then is your name really Shy Dove?"*

*She felt a sense of panic but knew there was no way she could not tell the truth now.*

*"Yes," she said, her chin raised in defiance.*

*"I have heard of a couple named Shy Dove and Running Deer who left their village under the cover of darkness. She was promised in marriage to the trader Eagle Feather's son, Broken Wing, who has also disappeared. Her village looked for them for many weeks before giving up. Her parents have been shamed that their daughter violated their agreement."*

*Shy Dove began to cry, overcome with the idea that she had caused her parents such trouble.*

*Horse Spirit's voice softened as he continued, "But even more, they grieve for the daughter they loved and believe they have lost."*

*This only made Shy Dove cry even harder, and she turned and ran back to the cave. Horse Spirit was not sure if he should follow her, but it had not been his intent to cause her pain. After waiting a few minutes to let her vent her feelings, he followed her to the cave. He found her inside on her sleeping blankets, curled in a fetal position, but her sobs had stopped. He knelt beside her and turned her around to take her in his arms. At first she resisted, but then the overwhelming feeling of grief at all she had lost took hold once again and she wrapped her arms around his neck and let her tears flow. He held her close to him and let her empty herself of her sadness, rubbing her back to calm her and murmuring words of comfort. Even after her sobs stopped, he continued to hold her and at last she pushed gently away from him, wiping her eyes. He held her face in his hands and kissed her gently on the lips. She did not know if she should return his kiss, but her emotions were too strong and she kissed him gently at first and then with more intent, letting him know she welcomed his touch. He sat back on his heels, still holding her face, and brushed a wisp of hair away from her face.*

*"I'm sorry, Cactus Blossom, or should I call you Shy Dove?" he asked.*

*"You are right. I am that same Shy Dove, or I was. I would like to be called Cactus Blossom now. That girl is no longer here. I can never go back to that life, and it is best that my parents and the others in my village think I am gone forever."*

*"I think I understand," he said. "I knew Broken Wing and although his father is not of the same temperament, it would be even harder for you and your family if he knew you were still alive. They have told themselves that you must be dead since no one has come to their village and told them they have seen any of you. Is what you told me about Running Deer's death true?"*

*"Yes," she said. "He was killed by a mountain lion not long after we arrived here. I was nearly dead myself, but from the sadness I felt. I was all alone and knew I could never return to my village. I'd thought that I would be alone for the rest of my life. And then you came," she said, looking into his eyes.*

*"What of Broken Wing?" he asked.*

*She took a deep breath before answering. "We had been traveling at night and sleeping during the day for several days. Running Deer wanted to put as much distance as possible behind us and thought that it would be safer to travel at night. We had thought we were finally safe when Broken Wing found us. He attacked Running Deer, and they struggled, but in the end, Running Deer killed Broken Wing. He was protecting me. If Broken Wing had found me, he would have killed me for having shamed him. He had already treated me unkindly even before we left, and I knew I could never be his wife even if I hadn't already been in love with Running Deer."*

*"I believe you. I did not know him well, but I saw enough of his actions to know that he was an arrogant man who thought that everyone should treat him as though he was special. He could be cruel if he thought he was being crossed."*

*"Will you tell anyone that you have found me?" she asked.*

*"No, I will not," he said.*

*A sense of relief filled her, and she knew she could believe him.*

*"I need to leave to return to my village, but I will be back soon. We can talk more about this and perhaps you could think about whether you would want to come with me the next time. How long do you want to be here by yourself? It isn't safe and as I told you, it is only a matter of time before someone else who may not be as friendly finds you."*

*"But what would I say about how I came to be here? If you found out, someone else could as well," she said.*

*"That is true," he considered. "Let me think about this.*

*Perhaps we can come up with a story that would make everyone believe it is true. I promise I will be back soon."*

*They walked together to his horses and Horse Spirit finished his packing before taking her in his arms one last time before leaving.*

*Shy Dove watched until he was out of sight. Shadow had followed for a short distance, as though escorting him away, and then turned and trotted back to her side.*

*"I think we both will miss him, won't we, Shadow?"*

*He barked his agreement before licking her hand and they both turned and returned to the place that was their home. Shy Dove hoped that Horse Spirit's promise to return soon would be kept. Hearing about her parents had filled her with sadness and guilt that being by herself was even harder to bear. She thought of his offer to leave with him and go to his village. Perhaps it was time to reconsider staying even though it meant leaving Running Deer, and she headed toward his grave, hoping to find some peace in whatever decision she would need to make.*

# CHAPTER FORTY-TWO

The next weaving session began the week after Sharon returned, and she couldn't wait. Her last project had turned out well, and the teacher had told her she was a natural. This time she wanted to do a more advanced design and, after the dream of Shy Dove's blanket, had sketched out a rough drawing of the image she'd had in the dream. She took it with her to show it to her instructor to ask for her advice about whether it would be too advanced or if it was even possible to do.

"It won't be easy, but I think you can manage it," she told Sharon. "It's an interesting combination of a more traditional tapestry style but has the Native American elements in it as well. How did you ever come up with this design?"

"It came to me in a dream," Sharon said.

The instructor continued to look at the sketch and Sharon knew from her own experience that the wheels were turning in her mind to deconstruct the design to figure out the techniques that would be needed to turn the drawing into the finished weaving.

"I think I've got it," she told Sharon and together they

worked out the steps to take and wrote them in on Sharon's sketch to use as a reference.

"What's that you've got?" Donna asked when she joined them.

Sharon showed her the sketch with the shapes and birds flying above a mountain range in the center of the drawing.

"This is going to be my next project," she told her.

"Wow, that's ambitious, but it will be beautiful. I think I'm going to stick to just trying to do another rug like we did last time. It came out okay, but I'd like to improve my skills."

"You're not giving yourself enough credit," Sharon told her.

"I think I'm giving myself more credit than I deserved," Donna chuckled.

"We are our own worst critics sometimes. I think you're seeing all the mistakes and not enough of the beauty in what you did."

"Thank you. On that note, I'm going to take the praise and go pick out materials to start Donna's Rug version 2.0."

Sharon joined her to pick out the wool she would need, eager to get started and hoping what was in her head would translate to the finished product. By the end of the class, she had her loom warped and started the actual weaving, feeling the excitement that always came when she had grasped a new skill.

"Do you have time to check out the new juice shop? They have acai bowls that are to die for! You can fill me in on your trip to Maine." Donna asked.

"That sounds terrific. Why don't I just follow you there and then I can head home once we're done."

Five minutes later, they were at the shop and had placed their orders.

"So, tell me all about the proposal," Donna prompted.

"It was so sweet. We were all in tears by the end of it—well, not Scott and Michael, although I think Scott may have come close once Jess broke down. Here, let me show you some pics. I totally forgot to take any during the actual proposal, but I have some after she accepted and he gave her the ring."

"Ooohhhh, what a great couple!" Donna exclaimed. "They're going to make a picture-perfect bride and groom. Have they set a date?"

"Just June for now. They need to make sure they can find a location for the reception, which shouldn't be too difficult as they want to keep it limited to close friends and family. A lot of places will have already been booked, but they're hoping with the guest size they can find a small banquet room at a hotel. They want to pay for it themselves, which is another reason to keep it small."

"That's nice. Sometimes those big weddings can get out of hand. They'll have the people there for whom it will mean the most."

"Very true," Sharon agreed. "I just wish for Jess's sake that Tom was still alive. She would so have liked for him to walk her down the aisle."

"Will she have someone else?" Donna asked.

"She's thinking about walking by herself," Sharon said.

"Would she have you walk her down instead?"

"I don't think she thought of that. I know I hadn't," Sharon said, considering that as a possibility and whether it would be something she would want to do. Certainly if Jess asked her, she would be glad to do it but wasn't sure if it was something she would suggest.

"And how did Mandy take it?" Donna asked.

"She was great about it. I looked over after Scott had proposed and she was crying, too, but I didn't detect even a hint of jealousy. She and Mandy are really close, and I think she knew this was coming just as I did, so it wasn't like she hadn't had time to prepare for it. It really was more about it being a matter of when, not if, they would get married."

"Do you think now she'll be more serious about her relationship with Michael, or should that be will Michael be more serious with Mandy?"

Sharon chuckled.

"Perhaps a little of each. They're both ambitious and career-oriented, but I have the feeling they both want children and they're not getting any younger. I know women wait longer than they used to but there are still arguments for not putting it off too long."

"Will you have time to find a dress when you get back or will you be buying one here?"

"Would you believe I really hadn't even thought of that? I think it makes more sense to find one here, but then I'll have to take it back with me. That still makes more sense, though. If I wait too long, I might not find something I like. Hmmm…. I think we have a shopping trip to do."

"Always happy to help," Donna said.

# CHAPTER FORTY-THREE

Sharon decided to wait to do the dress shopping when Mandy and Jessica came to visit in February. They had planned the trip even before the proposal, but the wedding planning gave them another reason to get together. Sharon picked them up at the airport, excited to finally be sharing her Arizona home with them. They had not been able to coordinate a trip the year before because of the girls' work schedules, so this was their first time visiting. Sharon was glad that she'd had a casita built for the times when out-of-town guests came to visit. It had two bedrooms, a full bathroom and an open concept living and kitchen/dining area. The kitchen itself did not have a stove, so they would be sharing meals in the main house. After taking them to the casita to drop their luggage, she gave them the tour of the main house before fixing a snack and drinks to enjoy on the patio.

"I could really get used to this," Jessica sighed, lounging in one of the chaises. "It was 10 degrees when we left Bangor this morning. Granted, it was before dawn, but it was only supposed to get to 20 degrees for the high."

"You may have to force us to leave," Mandy teased.

"I would love nothing more than for you to stay with me," Sharon disagreed. "I have a feeling that Scott and Michael might have something to say about it, though."

The girls both laughed.

"You may be right," Mandy said.

"You're definitely right," Jess agreed.

"I thought we might just take it easy the first day or two so you can get settled in unless you're up for more sooner," Sharon said.

"I should be back up to speed by tomorrow," Jess said.

"Me, too," Mandy chimed in.

"I do have something more serious I wanted to ask," Sharon said hesitantly, hoping she wasn't rushing things.

The girls looked at each other, not sure what to expect, and then turned to Sharon, awaiting her question.

"I'd like you to meet Joseph. He suggested we meet at a restaurant first to be in neutral territory and then, hoping it all goes well, he'd like to have us meet for dinner at his house so you can meet his son and daughter."

The girls exchanged another look.

"This sounds serious, Mom," Mandy said.

"I'm just trying to do things right this time. We are still going slow and haven't taken it beyond a committed, monogamous friendship so far," Sharon was saying, but stopped when she saw the smirks on their faces.

"So, you're telling us there haven't been any benefits so far?" Mandy teased her.

Sharon's face reddened.

"That is not something a lady discusses," she said primly but could not maintain the expression for long and chuckled while wagging her finger at them.

"Seriously, though, both Joseph and I want you to be okay with this. I learned the hard way that even though it is my life and my choices, it doesn't make for happy choices if the others you love are not on board."

"We want you to be happy, too, Mom," Jess said. "It wasn't ever about us wanting you to give that up with Hal. I guess we just saw in him what you couldn't. We finally got it about why you and Dad tried to warn us about certain friends when we were growing up, but you still let us learn on our own for the most part."

"That's exactly it," Mandy agreed. "Hal set off all the alarms and red flags and I am sorry that I was probably a lot ruder about it than I should have been. In the end, though, I'm glad you're not with him now. I hope it will be different with Joseph. You've seemed a lot happier the past few months and I think he's had something to do with that, so that's a good sign."

"You won't have long to find out. We made reservations for dinner tomorrow night just in case you were okay with the suggestion to meet."

"Looking forward to it," Jess told her, and Mandy nodded in agreement.

That settled, they spent the rest of the afternoon enjoying the sunshine and each other's company and making plans for a shopping trip the following day.

## CHAPTER FORTY-FOUR

They met Joseph the next night at the restaurant. Sharon's anxiety had been growing as the time approached, but she was hoping for the best. He had arrived ahead of them, and the hostess led them to the table where he was waiting. Seeing them approaching, he rose to greet them.

"Joseph Ramos, I'd like to introduce you to my daughters, Jessica and Amanda. Girls, this is Joseph Ramos."

"Very nice to meet you, ladies. Your mother has had nothing but good things to say about you both. And congratulations, Jessica," Joseph said.

"Thank you. It's very nice to meet you, too," Jess said, shaking hands with him.

He turned to shake Mandy's hand as well as she told him, "Nice to meet you. Mom has told us a little about you, but maybe you can tell us more."

"Well, you probably know that I own the construction company that built your mom's house, and that's how we met. I had the pleasure of meeting your dad, too, and I'm very sorry for your loss. He was a good man."

Sharon could see that this impressed the girls.

"I have a son named Peter who works in the construction company with me and a daughter, Melinda, who has two children of her own. My wife, Susan, passed away a little over five years ago and until I got to know your mom more after she spent last winter here, I didn't think I'd have any interest in dating, much less getting into a serious relationship with another woman. She's changed my mind, though, and I hope you'll find me worthy of her company."

"We're willing to give you a chance," Mandy said, "which is why we're here tonight. Did you ever meet Hal?"

"I did," he said with a wry expression.

"I take it you weren't impressed," Jess said.

"You could say that," he answered.

"Then you've already scored brownie points," Mandy said, smiling.

Sharon, meanwhile, was quiet but looking mortified by all the questioning.

"It's okay, Mom," Mandy said. "He's passed the first test. We'll back off now."

Joseph winked at Sharon to let her know he wasn't upset.

"What are you girls up to while you're here?" he asked, to turn the conversation to other topics.

Sharon looked relieved that they could move on.

"Tomorrow we're going into Tucson to do some sightseeing and possibly shopping for a dress for me for the wedding. This is the girls' first visit to Tucson, even though Tom and I used to come here on vacation for several years before we decided to build the house. We were only here for a couple weeks at a time, and they had their own things they were doing, so it just never came up. We're going to meet Donna for lunch so she can get a chance to meet them, too."

"Sounds like fun. Be sure to visit the Presidio district. How long are you here?"

"We could only take a week this time," Jess told him.

"I have a big case coming up that I'll need to prepare for, and Jess wants to save her time off for the honeymoon," Mandy explained.

"That's right. Your Mom told me you're an attorney and so is your boyfriend. Michael, isn't it?"

"I'm impressed," Mandy told him.

"I told you she's been telling me about you and it's obvious how proud she is of both of you," he said, addressing each of them.

"Tell us about your grandchildren," Jess redirected the conversation.

"Ahhh, they're the love of my life. All the stories about grandchildren being special are true. I'd thought other grandparents were exaggerating, but they were right. Joseph, but we call him Joey, is 7 years old and smart as a whip. Maya is 5 years old and the prettiest little thing you've ever seen. Melinda and her husband, David, have done a great job parenting. I've seen too many young parents these days who are afraid to make their kids mind their manners, but that hasn't been the case with them. Joey and Maya are some of the politest grandchildren I've ever seen, although I may be just a bit prejudiced."

"Maybe just a little," Jess teased.

"I haven't seen them often, but I have to say I've been impressed with them, too," Sharon agreed. "You're not just being prejudiced. They're great grandkids. I hope to have some of my own someday soon," Sharon teased, knowing that would probably get a rise out of both Jess and Mandy. She wasn't wrong.

"*Mom!*" Mandy said, pretending to be outraged but not able to hold it together before breaking out in a big smile. "Pressure's on you, big sister."

"No pressure at all," Jess replied. "Scott and I have already talked about wanting to get pregnant on our honeymoon, so joke's on you."

"I'm going to hold you to that. I'm not getting any younger, you know, and precious time is being wasted for spoiling grand-children," Sharon said.

The conversation was going well, she thought with more relief than she'd expected. Perhaps she'd been nervous for no reason. This was going much better than their interactions with Hal. She hoped it was a good sign of things to come. They still had to introduce the girls to Joseph's family, but if they were as accepting of them as they had been with her, she knew she would have no reason to worry. They lingered after finishing their dinners and desserts, enjoying the banter and the wait staff did not appear to be in any hurry to rush them off, but the time came for them to call it a night.

"It was so nice to meet you, Joseph," Mandy was the first to say.

"That goes for me, too," Jess agreed.

"The pleasure was all mine. I hope that means you'll accept my invitation to come to dinner on Friday. It's a family dinner, so my kids and grandkids will be there, but I want you all to meet each other. It's important to me and Sharon that we have your blessing. Yours and my kids, too."

"We'd love, to," they said in unison.

Once they were back at Sharon's house, they gathered in the living room with a glass of wine and lit the fireplace.

"He's really nice, Mom," Mandy said.

"I agree," Jess chimed in.

"I can't tell you how relieved that makes me," Sharon said. "I really think you're going to like Peter and Melinda and David. Joseph wasn't just bragging about his grandkids, either. They really are sweet."

"Looking forward to it," Jess said.

They drank their wine while talking about what they'd do the next day before calling it a night. The girls went to the casita and Sharon, completely relaxed now between the wine and having spent a great evening with her favorite people, headed to bed.

# CHAPTER FORTY-FIVE

They were up a little later than they'd planned, but after a quick breakfast, headed to Tucson for their sight-seeing expedition and dress shopping.

"I can't tell you how great it is to not be wearing a winter coat and boots!" Mandy exclaimed.

"I know, right?" Sharon replied.

"I'm very jealous, Mom," Jess told her. "You get to spend the entire winter away from all of that."

"Well, it took me a lot of years of working before I earned that right."

"You deserve every bit of what you have now," Jess said. "You'll be our inspiration for what we can aspire to having someday, too."

They did the tour of the Presidio and investigated the shops in the downtown section that morning before meeting Donna for lunch.

Introductions made; they found a table.

"You girls are just as beautiful as I expected," Donna told them.

"I guess Mom's been bragging us up again, huh?" Jess asked smiling.

"It's not a brag if it's true," Sharon cut in.

The girls looked at each other and rolled their eyes.

"Mom tells us you've been taking a weaving class together this year. You met taking the gourd class last winter, wasn't it?" Mandy asked.

"Yes, we hit it off right away, and it's made it so much nicer being here. I'm a transplant from Washington State and hadn't been here that long either when we met. I missed her like crazy last summer, though. Are you sure she can't just stay here all year long?" Donna joked.

"I'd never survive the summers," Sharon told her. "I don't care how dry the heat is, hot is hot and when it gets much past 90, I've met my tolerance. You'll never get me to give up Maine summers and even autumn is more enjoyable now that I know I don't have to stay there for winter."

"Tell me all about your wedding plans." Donna turned her attention to Jess. "Sharon said you're going to try to find her a dress while you're here?" she went on.

"That's right. We figured it would be easier to do that. Honestly, I'm not that fussy and anything she picked out would be fine by me, but she wanted to have my input."

"You say that now, but you never know. I might have thrown all abandon to my sensible side and shown up in some split up the side number that would have put you to shame."

"I cannot imagine that ever happening," Mandy said.

"Don't tempt her!" Jess joked.

Sharon smiled at them, thoroughly enjoying the banter.

"Do you know of any dress shops here that we might try?" Sharon asked.

"There are the malls, of course, and you already know about those, but there is a little boutique called Anni's Closet you might try. It can be hit or miss, but what they have is reasonably priced and the quality is good." Donna said.

They looked up the address online so that Sharon could put it into her Maps app before finishing up their lunch and saying their goodbyes.

"What do you think, should we try the boutique first?" Sharon asked.

"Yes, definitely!" Jess said. "The malls are more likely to have the same sort of thing you can find anywhere and for a wedding, it should be something a little more unique."

That settled, she brought up the address and entered it into the car's GPS. They found it with no problems and were pleased to find a convenient parking spot.

"This must be our lucky day!" Sharon announced after they'd found the perfect dress in her size that would not even need any alterations.

"It's perfect for you, Mom," Jess told her, admiring Sharon's reflection.

"I love it!" Mandy agreed. "Now if you can pick a maid of honor dress that's this nice, I'll be overjoyed."

"I'll do my best," Jess said, debating whether to tease her sister about finding one that would live up to the memes about bridesmaids' dresses.

Their missions accomplished, they headed back to Wilmont before the afternoon commute traffic began and to give themselves time to spend being lazy in the afternoon sunshine.

# CHAPTER FORTY-SIX

It had been a fun week for everyone, and Sharon hoped that this evening's dinner with Joseph's family would go smoothly. If the previous dinner with him was any indication, she had nothing to worry about, but she was still feeling nervous. They'd brought a bottle of wine and arrived at the appointed time. She saw from the cars in the driveway that Peter and Melinda's family were already here. Joseph greeted them at the door and welcomed them in.

"How have you been enjoying your time here?" he asked Jess and Mandy. "I thought about calling but didn't want to interrupt your visit."

"It's been great," Mandy told him. "I can see why Mom and Dad loved it here and now that I have a place to stay, I think I'll be coming more often."

"That goes for me, too," Jess echoed.

"You're welcome any time you want to come," Sharon said.

"Everyone's out on the patio. Come on in and I'll introduce you," Joseph told the girls.

They followed him out and Joseph made the introductions to

Melinda's family and Peter, who had brought his girlfriend, Nicole.

"Welcome to Arizona," Peter told them.

"Thanks. Everyone has been so kind to us, we feel like family," Jess said and blushed as she realized that may have been a faux pas considering the circumstances.

"Well, we love your mom, so you're already like family to us," Melinda told them, and it was Sharon's turn to blush as she had no idea she'd made that good of an impression.

Joseph put his arm around Sharon's shoulders and whispered in her ear, "I think you've got a fan."

She smiled up at him and relaxed, feeling that the evening was going to go well. She wasn't wrong as everyone got along as though they already knew each other. It was a happy group that left Joseph's house and headed back to Sharon's.

"Mom, I really like Joseph and his family," Mandy told her.

"Me, too. You've got my thumbs up," Jess chimed in.

"You don't know how happy that makes me," Sharon said. "I really didn't want to have a repeat of the Hal experience, and it means a lot to me that you both like Joseph and his family. This feels different with him. More like it's a relationship that is based on similar values."

"I think that's it. He feels like a much better match for you. Hal was too…. smarmy," Jess said, and gave Mandy a conspiratorial look.

"Did you teach her that?" Sharon asked Mandy, who just laughed.

"I did, but it still fits, don't you think?" Mandy replied.

Sharon just rolled her eyes.

They arrived home and headed to the living room for their final evening together, reluctant to just head to bed, knowing that they'd be saying goodbye in the morning.

# CHAPTER FORTY-SEVEN

*Horse Spirit returned a week later. Shy Dove had been nervous after his departure. She trusted him but was still worried that someone else would not be as understanding about her story about Broken Wing's death and might make her return to her own village. He put those worries to rest, though.*

*"I have told no one about you," he said. "I would like to take you to my village, though, and I think it would be best if I tell them I met you in another village and have taken you for my wife."*

*Shy Dove's mouth dropped. This was not at all what she had expected to hear.*

*"Hear me out. If you are my wife, no one will be able to force you to return to your village. We can introduce you as Cactus Blossom and that will be your name from now on. No one will connect you with the Shy Dove and Running Deer who are missing. It's not likely anyone from my village would ever learn that story as I only found out because I am a trader and had been in your village to trade. I will never tell them so there would be no problem."*

*Shy Dove considered the possibility and found that she was not as unwilling to accept the offer as she might have been even a month ago. She'd come to cherish the visits from Horse Spirit and the thought of spending the rest of her life alone with only occasional visits from him brought her almost as much sadness as Running Deer's death. It would be too much to bear, and she was still young. She wanted children and to have love in her life again, as well as to belong to a family.*

*Horse Spirit had been watching her face, lost in thought, as he waited for her to reply. He was worried that she would reject his offer, but he did not want to leave her here alone for even another day. If his first argument had not convinced her, he would have to come up with something else. Just as he was about to try again, she looked up at him with a determined expression on her face.*

*"I will go with you," she told him, "if you will promise me I can come back here if your family and the others in your tribe do not treat me well. I admit I am lonely, but I would rather live alone than be shunned. That would make the loneliness that much worse."*

*He let out his breath. "No one will shun you.... but I promise I will do as you ask," he hurried on when he saw that she was about to object.*

*"Could we stay here for just a little longer?" she asked. "I'm not quite ready to leave yet. This has been my home for the past few months, and I've already had to leave the village where I grew up without being able to say goodbye to my family. I have no family other than Running Deer here, and I have only his spirit to speak to, but do you understand?"*

*He could see the anguish on her face and didn't want to rush her. There was no reason to be back in his village at any particular time, and perhaps this would be better if they could spend time together. They had been together many times now, but never for very long. It would also help to prepare their story of how they met so that their stories would match if she was asked.*

*"Of course," he answered. "I think it best if I stay here with you and we practice the story we should tell anyone if they ask about you. From this day, I will only call you Cactus Blossom. That will be your name from now on and you will need to be sure to only answer to that."*

*"Yes, that makes sense," she said. "Does anyone else in your village speak my language?"*

*"How could I not have thought of that before? I am so used to speaking with you in your language that I forgot. I am the only one, but you will need to learn my language so that you can speak with others. I can teach you some now or we can wait until you can speak the language fluently before going to my village. I can stay with you here in the meantime."*

*She thought about this. She had almost been ready to leave sooner, but the fear of going to live with people she did not know and having to fit into their ways overtook her.*

*"Could we wait until I am more ready?" she asked.*

*"I will wait as long as you need, but there will be times when I will have to leave you alone so as not to cause suspicion."*

*"Yes, I understand, but I think that will be best. I have learned to be on my own with Shadow's help, so I am not afraid to be left. Right now, I am more afraid about going to your village."*

*"Then we should begin now to teach you my tongue," he said as he smiled at her.*

*He began as a parent would teach their young child to learn to talk by pointing to an object and saying the name and she would then repeat it. She was a quick study and by the end of the day, she could already remember several words. This might not be as difficult as she feared, and the excitement of being among people again encouraged her to keep going.*

# CHAPTER FORTY-EIGHT

Sharon had held it together, so it hadn't been a tearful goodbye at the airport, but now that she was alone, the tears fell slowly down her cheeks as she headed back to Wilmont. They had had so much fun during the week, and she felt like she had her girls back again. The summer had been filled with tension, but that was gone now. She wiped the tears away and realized there was no need to be sad. The wedding planning was going great and with her dress approved by the bride, she could relax and help when she could, but otherwise, it was in Jess and Scott's hands now. As the bride's family, she would put together the rehearsal dinner but the arrangements for that could be made by phone and internet. How did we ever manage things before, she thought.

The house felt empty after having had the girls here with her all week, but she was determined not to let the sadness overtake her. She needed something to keep her mind occupied, and the weaving project was just the thing to do that. Before long, it caught her in its spell. It had been challenging, but with her instructor's help, she had been turning the drawing into reality. It was a replica of the blanket she'd seen in her dream, but on a much smaller scale. This would become a wall hanging. She was so involved that she almost did not hear the phone ringing, but just as it was about to go to voice mail, she heard the ring tone and picked up.

"Oh, you are home," Joseph said. "I was just about to leave a message for you."

"Sorry, I almost didn't hear it at all as I was working on my weaving," she said.

"I thought you might want to hear a friendly voice after dropping the girls off at the airport."

"How do you know me so well?" she asked, and he could feel the smile on her face.

"Just a feeling," he said. "How about I get some takeout and bring it to your house for dinner, so you don't have to eat alone tonight?"

"That sounds wonderful," she said. "I really would love to have the company and even though we've seen each other, I've missed having one-on-one time with you."

"Me, too, and now that we've gotten the seal of approval from our respective kids, maybe we could have a conversation about how we go from here. I know where I'd like it to go, but I'm not going to assume that's how you feel, too."

"In this case, you are assuming correctly if you think I want to take it to the next level. Or am I the one who's assuming incorrectly?" she asked.

"Next level sounds just about perfect to me."

After settling on a time and restaurant for takeout, they said their goodbyes and feeling much happier, Sharon went back to her weaving.

# CHAPTER FORTY-NINE

Joseph arrived with the takeout order and beer, which they took to the kitchen to eat.

"How did your weaving go?" he asked.

"It's a challenge, but I'm enjoying that. I get bored quickly with projects that are too easy, so if that's the criteria, let's just say I don't think I'll ever get bored with this one."

"Keeps you sharp," he replied.

"Would you like to see it?" she asked.

"I would and I'm not just saying that," he said as she seemed to be judging whether he was just being polite.

She led him into her craft room where she had the loom. The rug was about two-thirds done and she had just finished the detail of the birds and was finishing up the mountains in the background that made up the tapestry section. Joseph whistled in appreciation.

"Sharon, this is incredible!"

"Thanks! I'm really pleased with how it's turning out."

"You're quite the artist. I thought your gourd projects were something special, but I think you've found your calling with the weaving," he told her.

"It does feel like it's coming naturally to me. There's just something about seeing it come to life that makes me happy."

"Then I hope you keep up with it. It would be a shame to waste your talent."

"I do plan to, even if I don't keep taking classes. The classes are fun, though, and it gives me an excuse to spend time with Donna. Not that I need an excuse, but I guess it's more that we make a point of getting together that way. I've never been very good at being the one to initiate contact with my friends, and sometimes even my family. It's not that I don't care about them, but my introvert nature takes over and before I know it, more time has passed than I intended without reaching out."

"I get that. I can be like that, too," he said.

"Why don't we light a fire, and you can tell me about your day," Sharon suggested.

"Not that much to talk about, but I like the idea of the fire and just being with you," he answered.

They snuggled on the couch and the fire's dancing flames soon relaxed them as they chatted about Joseph's day while holding hands.

"This is nice," Sharon said as she laid her head on his shoulder and he removed his hand to put his arm around her shoulders to tuck her closer to him.

He raised her chin to make it easier to kiss her lips.

"That was even nicer," he said.

She closed her eyes and kissed him again, her lips parting and her breath hitching as he returned the kiss. His fingers wound in her hair, and he turned his body slightly to embrace her and then pulled back.

"Is it time to have that talk about where we go from here?" he asked.

She reluctantly sat up and faced him.

"Yes, I do," she agreed.

"I think we've already established that we're dating and

maybe going steady," he joked. "I didn't think I could feel this way about anyone except Susan, but never say never strikes again. My kids think you're terrific and I think your kids like me, too."

"They do," Sharon agreed, "and they really like your family. I got their thumbs up when we came back from your dinner."

"In that case, no more waiting?" he asked, looking her in the eyes.

She smiled and said, "No more waiting."

He stood and took her hand to pull her up to walk into her bedroom. She flipped the switch that turned on the lamp on her nightstand, which she already had on a dimmer so that the room was lit with a soft glow rather than the bright overhead.

"I like what you've done with it," he said.

She was surprised at first since, after all, he had built it, but then realized he hadn't been in her bedroom since she'd decorated the house and added the furniture.

"Thanks. I hope you'll like my choice for a mattress," and then groaned. "That was a bit over the top."

"Not at all," he grinned. "I've been wondering for months how it would feel."

"Months?" she asked in surprise.

"I've been waiting for you to catch up with me since last spring when you left. It didn't feel to me like Hal was going to be in the picture for long, but I knew you had to find out for yourself that he wasn't right. It nearly killed me, but it was what I had to do."

She didn't know how to take this. She had had feelings for Joseph, too, but she did not know he'd felt this way about her.

He stroked her hair and kissed her, making a reply unnecessary. She felt his tongue teasing her lips apart and her body responded. He pressed his body closer, and she could tell how ready he was, which only increased her desire. She broke the embrace to sit on the bed and patted the space beside her in invitation to join her.

"I'm not as acrobatic as I was a couple of decades ago. I think it would be safer for both of us if we continued this down here," she said.

He smiled and sat down next to her.

"You're preaching to the choir. I'd just as soon not have to explain to anyone how I put out my back."

She smiled in agreement as she unbuttoned his shirt, revealing a body that was still in good shape for his age. His years of working in construction had kept his muscles toned, and she doubted that he would have had any difficulty continuing their lovemaking where they'd been, but she was just as happy to be on the bed. Comfort had its advantages, and she'd reached the time in her life where comfort over acrobatics took priority.

He slipped her blouse over her head and reached around to undo her bra. and she was glad to have the softer light, at least for their first romantic encounter. She was in good shape for her age, too, but gravity and the toll time had taken was still a factor and her embarrassment had kicked in. He put that to rest, though, by kissing her neck in that most sensitive of spots and she shivered as her eyes fluttered closed. His touch was gentle and slow but deliberate as he laid her back, and she pulled her legs up onto the bed as he laid down beside her. He unzipped her jeans, pulling her underpants along with them as he slid them down her legs and tossed them onto the floor. She sucked in her breath as he took one of her nipples in his mouth and stroked his hand down the other side of her body. He continued to bring her desire to the edge of climax and then retreating until she was begging for him to go on. At last, he undressed completely and held himself over her.

"Please, Joseph, I can't take much more," she told him, her breath ragged.

He entered her slowly, building up her desire to the point that she didn't think she could stand it. She wrapped her legs around him as he quickened his thrusts, and they both cried out as they climaxed in unison.

He pulled her over on her side as he rolled off her and held her in his arms and kissed the top of her head.

"That was amazing," he told her. "I think you took off a couple decades because I didn't think I still had that in me," he said, chuckling.

"I could say the same," she told him.

They lay wrapped in each other's arms and drifted off to sleep.

## CHAPTER FIFTY

"I'd ask how your weekend was, but I think I can guess it was a good one," Donna teased.

Sharon didn't even bother to feign ignorance about what Donna meant as she felt her face redden.

"And you would be right," was all she replied, but smiled, letting Donna know she didn't take offense at the jab.

They carried their looms and supplies to their usual spot for the weaving class, admiring each other's projects. Their instructor came over to examine their work and see if they needed any help before the rest of the class arrived.

"Sharon, this is remarkable for a beginning student. You really haven't done this before?" she asked, admiring her tapestry.

"Not in this lifetime," Sharon replied, although there was no way she was going to expand on her secret belief that she'd inherited her ability from a past lifetime.

"I hope you keep up even after this class is done. You have a natural talent and could really take this to another level." She turned to Donna, realizing she was leaving her out of the conversation. "Donna, you've made a lot of progress since our first class. I hope you keep up with weaving, too. I think you've got real potential to become a skilled weaver."

"I'll never be on Sharon's level, but I do want to keep weaving. It has almost a meditative quality to it and when I'm in the zone, I can let go of whatever else is causing chaos in my life."

The rest of the class filed in and the teacher excused herself to greet the other students.

"You know, I do expect to hear more about your weekend," Donna said.

"I figured I wasn't going to get off that easily," Sharon retorted. "Let's grab some lunch after class and I'll fill you in."

They found a restaurant nearby and headed to a booth in the back, where they would have more privacy.

"Sooooo, do tell," Donna encouraged after they had placed their order.

Sharon considered how much detail she wanted to get into before responding.

"Well, you know I've been dating Joseph, and the girls met him and his family while they were here. They all got along really well, so we thought that was a good sign that it would be okay to take things to the next level. Joseph spent the weekend with me, and it went really well," Sharon said, blushing.

"Sharon, I'm thrilled for you," Donna said, and Sharon knew she was sincere. "You went through a really rough patch the past year and you deserve to have some happiness in your life."

"Thanks," she said, the tears threatening to fill her eyes, and she blinked them away. "I'd thought I was happy when I first met Hal but now that I'm with Joseph, I realize just how much of a mistake that would have been to stay with him."

Donna reached over and put her hand over Sharon's. "We all make mistakes and trust the wrong people sometimes. I did that with my ex-husband instead of questioning his behavior sooner. I'm not trying to make it a contest," she reassured Sharon, "but if it was, you'd be the winner of that one. You caught on much sooner than I did and have no reason to feel any shame about what happened."

"That's just it. I've mostly told myself there's no reason to, but every so often it creeps in. I keep telling myself that I should have known better at my age, but maybe age is what made me even more vulnerable. Or at least in that situation."

"Well, that's over and done with and you've moved on. Time to let it go. You made a mistake, but you fixed it and learned from it. It's all part of life, isn't it?"

"Yeah, I guess so."

The conversation paused as the server arrived with their lunch orders.

"I just realized you've never really talked about your ex," Sharon said.

"He was a compulsive gambler who managed to hide his addiction, although I didn't find out until the last year of our marriage just how bad it was or even that's what it was that was the cause for the late nights and mood swings. To be honest, I'd thought it was affairs and just never had the guts to come out and ask. I was one of those wives who stuck it out," she raised her hands to make air quotes, 'for the kids' even after they were grown."

"I'm sorry you had to deal with that," Sharon told her.

"The thing is, I'm not so sure that it actually was better for the kids. I learned after the fact they're a lot more aware than we give them credit for sometimes. There was a lot of tension that was obvious even though we thought because we didn't fight in front of them, they didn't know what was going on. Was that really better than being children of divorced parents if I could have been happier and given more of myself as quality time? It's a moot point now, but if I had it to do over…."

"My turn to tell you not to beat yourself up. I'm sure you did the best you could at the time, and you did what you thought was best for the sake of the kids. There's definitely no shame in that."

Donna smiled, her eyes shimmering with tears this time. She dabbed at them with her napkin and laughed nervously.

"Well, aren't we quite the pair? I thought we were supposed to be having fun and here we are making each other cry."

"That's what true friends are for, to be there for the sad times, not just the fun ones," Sharon said gently. "I'm lucky to have you as my friend."

"The feeling's mutual," Donna said. "We better change the subject, though, or we're going to be getting even more looks from the server than we already have."

Sharon looked over at the server, who quickly averted his glance, confirming Donna's assessment of the situation.

"I see what you mean. In that case, tell me about your neighbor. Has he given up yet?"

"I think he's taken it as a personal challenge to wear me down," Donna said, and rolled her eyes.

Sharon laughed and said, "He obviously does not know the depth of your stubbornness."

They both laughed, and the mood lightened. They finished their lunches with no more concerned looks from the server and made plans for Donna to visit later in the week.

## CHAPTER FIFTY-ONE

*Horse Spirit had spent two weeks with her teaching her his language and Cactus Blossom, as she now thought of herself, could speak in sentences with him. Her skills were still at a basic level, but she could communicate her needs and understand most what he spoke to her. Their feelings for each other were also growing and while Running Deer would always be the love of her life, she knew that Horse Spirit would treat her kindly and she could have a good life with him.*

*She was at her loom when he returned later that day. He and Shadow had bonded, and Cactus Blossom realized that Shadow had missed having a man to follow and take him on hunting excursions. Shadow trotted up to her, licking her face in greeting, and she laughingly pushed him away so that she could scratch his head to distract him from the face washing.*

*"How was your hunting trip?" she asked Horse Spirit.*

*He brought out two rabbits he had in the satchel on his back to show her.*

*"Shadow is an excellent tracker. It made it much easier to find them."*

*"We should reward him as well when we have our dinner later," she replied.*

*He looked appreciatively at the weaving she was working on and knelt on his haunches beside her to examine it.*

*"Your work is beautiful," he said.*

*"Thank you," she answered.*

*"And you are learning my language so easily. I think we will be ready to leave within another week."*

*Although she'd been expecting they would not stay here for long, she was still nervous about meeting new people. She had never ventured outside her own village before she and Running Deer left and the only strangers she'd met were the few traders and relatives of villagers who had come to visit.*

*Horse Spirit could see her apprehension and reached out to put his hand on her shoulder in reassurance.*

*"You will be fine," he told her. "Your language is improving every day and you know enough now to understand what is being said to you. Your ability to speak back will get better with prac-tice. You know the story we have come up with about how we met. There is nothing to be worried about."*

*"I hope so," she said, but not with conviction.*

*He bent down and kissed her lips. It was the first time he had shown such a physical gesture. It had been such a long time since she'd had any physical touch from another human being, and she realized how much she'd been missing it. Although it had provided warmth and comfort, having Shadow around her could in no way make up for another human touch.*

*Horse Spirit hesitated as she did not immediately return his kiss and was about to stand when she reached out and kissed him, holding the back of his head, and then turning so that she could embrace him with both arms. He reached around her waist and pulled her even closer to him. He stood, lifting her in his arms, and walked toward her cave, only putting her down as they reached the trail that led up the hill. Taking her hand instead, he continued the climb as she followed willingly. He led her to her sleeping blankets and pulled her down to sit beside him, taking her face in both hands and kissing her deeply. She felt the flutter of passion awaken once again as she returned his kisses. He pulled her tunic over her head and then laid her down on the blankets, pausing to look at her.*

*"You are so beautiful, Cactus Blossom. I have wanted this for so long. Are you sure you are ready? I don't want to rush you."*

*"I'm sure," she told him.*

*"This will be our joining and from this day forward you will be my wife," he said, but it was also a question.*

*"I take you as my husband, Horse Spirit," she said, letting him know she was agreeing to his question.*

*He pulled off his tunic and breeches and gently made love to her. For the first time since Running Deer's death, she once again felt loved and protected.*

* * *

SHARON WOKE from the dream and sighed. She'd wanted Shy Dove, now Cactus Blossom, to be happy and no longer alone, and it looked like that was finally going to happen.

# CHAPTER FIFTY-TWO

*"It's time, Cactus Blossom," he said gently.*

*"I know," she whispered in reply.*

*She had packed the items she knew she could not do without the day before and this morning had arisen with the sun to say her goodbyes to the place she had called home for the past year. Her goodbye to Running Deer had been the hardest. Although her grief had subsided to being a reminder rather than ever-present as the months had passed by, he would always be her first love. The dreams of the future that would never come to be with him were something she had to put aside. Her future now lay with Horse Spirit. She had come to love him, too, and knew that he felt the same way about her. With him, she had the possibility of children and a life shared with family and friends. At least she hoped they would accept her into his village, but that uncertainty had her hesitating to leave. Would it be even worse to be around others but still feel alone if they did not? There would be times when he would be gone for months while he was on his trading trips, so being accepted as one of them could make her life so much easier. If not, though, she could always come back here while he was away, she told herself. She had been on her own and done well so far. She could do it again if she had to.*

*"Cactus Blossom?"*

*"I'm ready," she said as she took a deep breath and climbed on Wind with his help. Stallion would carry his trade goods and the possessions she was bringing with her, so Horse Spirit was walking instead while Shadow trotted beside him.*

*The day was sunny, with sparse clouds breaking up the azure blue of the sky. It would soon become hot, but for now it was perfect and Horse Spirit hoped to make good time. He knew how hard it was for Cactus Blossom to leave, so had not wanted to push her before she was ready and was relieved they had gotten an early start. Not as early as it would have been if he had his way, but still early enough to make it to the spot where he would usually rest before going on the next day to his village. In the end, they had decided to keep things simple and only say that he had met her on his trading trip and they had married. No one in his village traveled far beyond the village itself and since he traded, they did not need to trade with others, so the chances of anyone having heard of Shy Dove and Running Deer were not likely. Changing her name to Cactus Blossom made it even less likely to make the connection and Shy Dove had made the decision to keep it to start her new life with him.*

*She was quiet as they made their way, wrapped up in her own thoughts of what awaited her and curiosity about the unfamiliar landscape before her. Horse Spirit would point out landmarks here and there that he used to navigate his way. She made a point of committing them to memory in the off chance that she would ever need to return this way on her own.*

*They made good progress and reached Horse Spirit's usual camp spot a couple hours before sunset, giving them time to unpack the horses and gather wood for a fire. There was a stream nearby to refill their water gourds and get drinks for themselves and the animals, as well as washing up.*

*"We made good time. Tomorrow we should be at my village by afternoon," he told her.*

*Cactus Blossom smiled at him, but Horse Spirit could see that she was trying to keep tears from falling. He took her chin in his hand and raised it so he could kiss her and stroked his other hand over her hair to reassure her.*

*"It will be alright," he told her, looking in her eyes so that she could see that he would make sure that happened.*

*"As long as you are with me, I have no doubt of that. It's when I will have to be by myself with the women in the village, that I am worried."*

*"It will be alright," he repeated, more forcefully this time.*

*She shook her head in agreement and smiled, hoping he was right.*

* * *

*THEY HAD MADE good time and reached Horse Spirit's village by mid-day of the following day, as Horse Spirit had hoped. It was smaller than Cactus Blossom's village, but she was feeling overwhelmed. It had been over a year since she'd been with more than one other person at a time and the sounds of children playing, the smells of different food being cooked than she was used to and simply seeing so many people again was almost more than she could handle. Even Shadow was being affected by all the strange sounds and smells and began to whine. Horse Spirit stroked his head to calm him and then realized that it was not just Shadow who needed comfort. He looked up to see Cactus Blossom sitting stiff and erect on Wind's back, staring at the scene before her and her face revealed the emotions and panic that had overtaken her.*

*"It is alright, Cactus Blossom," he said, putting his hand on her thigh to reassure her and bring her attention to him.*

*She startled and looked down at him as though coming out of a trance.*

*"I don't know if I can do this, Horse Spirit," she said as tears rolled down her cheeks.*

*"You can, and I will be with you. There is no need to be afraid. You are with me as my wife, and no one will harm you. No one has seen us yet so we can take a few minutes here to get the horses settled and give you time to prepare yourself to meet everyone."*

*She nodded in agreement and let him take her hand and put his other hand around her waist to help her down from Wind's back. Just then, another dog from the village spotted them and ran toward Shadow, barking. Shadow began barking and growling, not knowing if the greeting was friendly or a threat but determined to protect his humans if it was the latter. Any opportunity to make a quieter entrance was lost as the dogs alerted the villagers to their presence. The faces of the men who had come forward turned to smiles as they recognized Horse Spirit. The owner of the village's dog commanded him to stop barking and Horse Spirit did the same with Shadow. Two of the men greeted Horse Spirit with slaps on the back and hugs before looking at Cactus Blossom with obvious curiosity.*

*"Who is this?" the older man asked Horse Spirit.*

*"This is Cactus Blossom. My wife," he replied.*

*The man looked at him in surprise before turning back to Cactus Blossom.*

*"Welcome to our village," he said. His tone was kind, and she could see no threat in his eyes.*

*"Thank you," she said, hoping she had said it in their language correctly in her nervousness.*

*"This is my father, Black Wolf," Horse Spirit told her. "And this is my brother, Antelope."*

*"Welcome," the younger man told her, the curiosity on his face apparent.*

*"I met Cactus Blossom while on my trading trips and fell in love with her. It took me a few times to convince her to become my wife and move back with me, but I finally did. I hope the village will all treat her as one of our own," Horse Spirit said, his words carrying the meaning he intended.*

*Black Wolf nodded, acknowledging what Horse Spirit was saying.*

*"We should have a feast tonight to celebrate your return... and your marriage. I will make sure that message of welcome is given."*

*"My father is the chief of the village," Horse Spirit explained.*

*Cactus Blossom's surprise was apparent on her face. Horse Spirit had never mentioned this to her before. Perhaps this was why he was so sure that she would be accepted by the village, although she knew first she would have to earn her place with his family.*

*More people had come over, curious to see what was happening and who this new arrival was that Horse Spirit had brought with him, in addition to his other items for trade. A short, round woman with braids that fell to her waist approached and first gave Horse Spirt a hug and kiss on both cheeks before focusing her attention on Cactus Blossom, her eyes calculating.*

*"Mother, this is Cactus Blossom. My wife," he introduced her and took her hand in his. "Cactus Blossom, this is Dancing Stream, my mother."*

*Cactus Blossom felt the fear in her stomach, but Horse Spirit squeezed her hand and his strength flowed into her. She wasn't sure what would be the correct way to approach Dancing Stream but had to try something.*

*"It is my honor to meet you, Dancing Stream. I hope I will prove worthy and will do my best to be a help to your family."*

*Dancing Stream was quiet for a moment, looking into her eyes and taking in Cactus Blossom's words before finally approaching her and wrapping her arms around Cactus Blossom's shoulders.*

*"Welcome to our village and our family. I trust my son's judgment and if he feels you are someone who belongs in our family, then that is all I need."*

*Cactus Blossom let out her breath and returned the hug. Feeling the warmth of Dancing Stream's body and her welcome filled her with emotions. It had been so long since she had been without the comfort of family and friends and a sense of belonging, it was almost more than she could bear.*

*Dancing Stream took Cactus Blossom's hand and led her toward the village.*

*"Come, let me introduce you to some of the women in the village and let these men take care of the horses and Horse Spirit's goods. Horse Spirit, bring Cactus Blossom's things to our home first."*

*"Yes, Mother," he said, smiling at them both, knowing there was no point in arguing with his mother. His father might be the chief of the village, but his mother was the unspoken leader of their family.*

*"Have you eaten?" she asked Cactus Blossom, who shook her head. "Come then, I was just finishing up preparing our meal before my son so rudely interrupted me." She smiled, though, so that Cactus Blossom knew she was not truly angry.*

*As they walked back toward Black Wolf and Dancing Stream's house, which she realized would now be her house as well—at least until Horse Spirit could build them one of their own—Dancing Stream introduced Cactus Blossom to the other women in the village.*

*"Don't worry about remembering their names," Dancing Stream told her, knowing without being told that Cactus Blossom was becoming anxious. "It took me several months to learn the names when Black Wolf brought me here."*

*"You're not from this village?" Cactus Blossom asked in surprise.*

*"No, my child. Black Wolf brought me here much as Horse Spirit has brought you. I know the feelings you are having now," and she patted Cactus Blossom's hand.*

*Cactus Blossom's anxious look was replaced with a smile and in that moment, she knew she would be okay.*

* * *

*IT HAD BEEN seven months since they first came to the village, and they now had their own home. It was small but close to Black Wolf and Dancing Stream. Her arrival had been accepted by the villagers, not just because of the speech that Black Wolf had given at the feast for their arrival, but because of Cactus Blossom herself. Her easy-going nature and kindness and willingness to help when needed had made her integration into their community a natural fit.*

*Cactus Blossom stretched. She had been weaving for several hours already and, as always, the weaving had captured her in its spell. She reached over to pat Shadow's head and her other hand stroked over her round belly. Not long after they had arrived, Cactus Blossom had realized that it had been two months since her last bleeding. It was the first grandchild for Black Wolf and Dancing Stream, and if Cactus Blossom herself had not earned her welcome into their family, the news of their grandchild had cemented that. Horse Spirit had been bursting with pride when she'd told him, and his love for her had only grown. He had just arrived back from another trading trip the week before, wanting to make sure that he was here for their baby's arrival.*

*Cactus Blossom got up to relieve herself and felt a stab of pain as her stomach contracted. She realized now that she had been feeling this earlier, too, but was so caught up in her weaving that it was more like the annoyance of a fly landing on her skin that she swatted away without even thinking twice about it. She felt the liquid flowing down her legs and thought she had wet herself before she had time to get to the latrine. The next stab of pain, though, convinced her it was time for her baby to be born. She waited until the contraction passed, breathing instinctively to ease the pain, and went to find Dancing Stream.*

*Dancing Stream knew as soon as she saw Cactus Blossom's face and how she was holding her body that the time had come. She called out to a young girl nearby.*

*"Sage, run and find Desert Song. Cactus Blossom, come with me," and put her arm around Cactus Blossom's shoulder to lead her back to her house.*

*The labor went quickly for a first birth and within hours, Cactus Blossom and Horse Spirit were holding their baby boy.*

*"Welcome to our family," Cactus Blossom whispered as she held the swaddled bundle in her arms, looking into the eyes that were fixed on hers.*

*Horse Spirit was holding Cactus Blossom in his arms and reached out a finger to gently touch his son's cheek.*

*Cactus Blossom looked up at her husband, seeing the love and pride on his face.*

*"I love you, Horse Spirit."*

*He kissed her lips and told her, "I love you, too, Cactus Blossom. I will protect you and our son with my life. I promise you, you will never regret becoming my wife."*

*She knew his words were true. She thought again of how she had hoped to be living her life with Running Deer, but this was what the Great Spirit had planned for her instead.*

*"You are right, Horse Spirit, I never will."*

# CHAPTER FIFTY-THREE

The months had gone by quickly, and now it was time for Sharon to return to Maine. She and Joseph had become even closer, and they knew that this was a relationship that was meant to last.

"I'm going to miss you," Joseph told her when he dropped her at the airport.

"Me, too, but I'm excited about having you visit on my turf," she told him.

Sharon hadn't been sure if he'd want to come, but Jessica and Scott wanted him to be there for their wedding. It wasn't just Sharon and Joseph's relationship that had grown in the months since the girls visited her in Arizona. They had had frequent FaceTime calls with Sharon and Joseph as well and had accepted him with open arms. That feeling of having known him for much longer and instantly liking him had been the same for them. Sharon had a very good feeling about their future.

"I can't wait. I've never been to Maine, but it's been on my bucket list. It would never have happened had it not been for you and your girls, though."

He leaned down to give her a hug and kiss and she thought

back to their farewell a year ago when she'd seen his face morph into Running Deer's. So much had happened since then and although not all of it had been happy times, she wouldn't have changed a thing. Not even her relationship and breakup with Hal, she realized. It had made her appreciate Joseph even more.

"I'll call when I get in to let you know I made it home safe and sound."

"Sounds like a plan. Have a good trip!"

She wheeled her carryon behind her and headed inside, knowing he'd be doing the same in another week, making it easier to leave.

CHAPTER FIFTY-FOUR

he wedding day had finally arrived, and Sharon was nearly as nervous as Jessica. Jess and Scott had stuck to their plans for keeping the guest list small, which had made it possible to have the ceremony and reception at Sharon's house instead of a local banquet room, and although the details were simple, not everything had gone smoothly.

"No, the flowers are not what I'd ordered," Jess was telling the florist after having received the delivery and finding that the wedding bouquet was nothing like the photo she'd given them. "I'm sending you a photo… again… of what we'd discussed when I ordered the flowers back in January. When will you be able to get the correct one to me? We have four hours before the ceremony, but the photographer is taking photos now."

Her voice was calm but tinged with anger and Sharon knew this was the time to sit back and let her daughter handle it. Jessica rarely got angry, but when she did, watch out! Even Mandy had kept her distance and let her usually easy-going sister take the reins.

The hair and make-up stylist was finishing up, the photographer had arrived to take photos of the preparations, and the tent had been set up the night before. The gardens were not in as full bloom as she would have liked, but Jess didn't seem to mind. They had found a spot that would be lovely for photos, and the photographer had assured them she could film in a way that would minimize any bare spots.

"That's not good enough," Jess was saying, and Sharon and Mandy exchanged looks, both with eyebrows raised. This was not the Jess they knew and loved. Had she become Bridezilla?

"Mmm hmm. Fine, I'll send someone there to pick them up in an hour if delivery is your problem. And you have the picture I just sent you?" After a pause while the florist replied, she finished with, "Thank you. I'll have someone there within the hour." She disconnected the call and let out her breath.

"I'm impressed, Sis," Mandy told her.

Jess chuckled and seemed to relax.

"A little too Bridezilla?" she asked.

"Not at all," Sharon assured her. "They screwed up, and you didn't let them take advantage of the situation. I'm proud of you."

"Thanks, Mom. Do you think Michael could go get the flowers?" she asked Mandy.

"Sure, I'll call him now to let him know. Would you just text him that pic of the bouquet so he can check before he leaves the florist to make sure it's right?"

Jess picked up her phone and navigated through the places needed to do that and hit Send.

"I let him know you'll be calling him to explain," she told Mandy.

Jess turned to Sharon with a frown on her face, looking like she was working up the courage to ask her something.

"What is it, Jess?"

Jessica looked up and set her shoulders back, having made her decision to act.

"Do you think Joseph would walk me down the aisle?"

Sharon couldn't have been more surprised. This was not at all what she'd expected.

"I… I don't know, but we could ask him."

"Would you mind?" Jess asked. "I know we haven't known him long, and I'd always imagined Dad walking me down the aisle. It's just that he already feels like family, and it feels right. I can't explain it…," her voice trailed off.

Sharon smiled. "I think he would be honored. Let me go find him and bring him in so you can ask him yourself."

She returned a few minutes later with a confused Joseph, looking handsome in his suit.

"I just told him you had something you wanted to ask, but I didn't say what," Sharon told Jess as they came back into the room where she was waiting. "How about if I leave you two alone?"

"No, I want you to be here, Mom," Jess answered.

Joseph was looking even more confused as he looked from one to the other.

"It's a good thing," Jess assured him, smiling. "Or at least I hope it's a good thing. I'd like for you to walk me down the aisle. If you'd be willing to do that," she added. "I know this sounds a little crazy, but it feels like the right thing. I can see how much you love my mom and even though it's only been a few months since we met, you feel like family already. I'd be so honored if you would do this."

"Wow!" he took a deep breath and his eyes glistened with the emotion this had brought. "I'm the one who would be honored. Are you sure?"

"I'm sure," she said and walked to him and put her arms around his neck to give him a hug and he hugged her back. "Besides, I know you can dance after seeing you and Mom at the rehearsal dinner last night," she teased, trying to lighten the mood.

There were tears in everyone's eyes now and tissues passed around to blot them before the makeup was ruined for the ladies.

"You look beautiful, by the way," Joseph told her, smiling as he stepped back holding her hands in his.

Michael arrived an hour later with the correct bouquet and a message from the florist that he would refund the cost from the bill.

"The squeaky wheel gets the grease," Sharon told Jess.

Both Jess and Mandy groaned.

"Yes, Mom, we know. But I guess you were right, it worked," Jess replied.

Hours later, Sharon and Joseph were sitting at a table by themselves, holding hands and looking at the guests enjoying themselves on the dance floor.

"Thank you again for inviting me," he said.

She smiled up at him. "Thank you for coming. I couldn't imagine you not being here, but I'm happy to know that you've enjoyed it, too."

"It's made me realize… even more than I already thought… just how much I want to be a part of your… all of your…," he said looking over at Jess and Mandy with Scott and Michael on the dance floor, "lives." He hesitated before going on. "Sharon, this may not be the time or place, or maybe it's exactly the right time and place, but I want this to be forever. Would you marry me?"

Her mouth dropped open, and he smiled as he gently pushed it closed.

"I'm hoping that's not a bad sign."

She laughed despite herself and shook her head.

"No, no, it's not a bad sign. Yes, I'll marry you." She said and kissed him. "Let's wait until later to tell the girls, though. This is Jess and Scott's night."

"Of course. Now, may I have this dance?" he asked as he pulled her to her feet.

# EPILOGUE

They had waited until Jess and Scott returned from their honeymoon to make their announcement by video call so they could have Sharon and Joseph's families hearing it at the same time. Much to their relief, everyone was as excited as they were at the news.

The date for the wedding finally arrived. They had set it for January in Arizona. It had made the most sense to Sharon to have it there, as that was where she and Joseph had fallen in love. And rediscovered that love, Sharon thought to herself, the morning of their wedding day. Her dreams of Shy Dove/Cactus Blossom had stopped, but she felt in her heart that everything had turned out okay for them and now the cycle was coming full circle. She and Joseph/Running Deer were together once more.

Joseph had finally retired, handing the business over to Peter, but helping out occasionally. That way, he could spend the summer months with Sharon in Maine. They had also decided to make Sharon's house their home base in Arizona. It was the house that Joseph had built for her and felt like the right place to be. There had been some discussion with Peter and Melinda about giving up their childhood home, but in the end, Peter had bought it to keep it in the family and had moved in the month before.

They had kept the ceremony and reception simple, with just family and a few friends invited, which included Donna, of course. Donna and her plus one, Gary Phillips, the neighbor who had finally worn her down.

"I guess we both should never say never," Sharon teased her, as they had a moment alone.

Donna sighed. "I know. What can I say, he was persistent."

They both chuckled, knowing her protestations were not believed by either of them.

"I'm so happy for you, Sharon," she said, serious now.

"Me, too," Sharon said, looking over at Joseph. He was in conversation with Peter but looked up as though he had sensed her eyes upon him and smiled at her.

"Me, too," she repeated softly.

# DISILLUSIONED DREAMS

Donna Mackenzie has had a good life living in Seattle with her husband, Richard "Dick" Mackenzie and their grown sons, John and Brian. That is, until Dick's gambling addiction comes to light, with devastating consequences for his business as an investment advisor and their family.

Deciding her life needs a fresh start, she quits her job, sells her house, and moves to Tucson, Arizona. She quickly makes friends with snowbird, Sharon Peterson, at a gourd crafting class and settles into her new routine.

What she has no interest in is becoming involved in another romantic relationship. She's convinced she can never trust a man again. Her newly divorced neighbor at her condo complex, Gary Phillips, has also had bad luck with his marriage. His instant attraction to Donna has him rethinking his resolution to not become romantically involved. Persuading Donna to trust enough to love again may be the biggest challenge he's ever had, but he's determined it's one he'll win. Donna finds Gary's overtures annoying. How can someone be so dense about taking a hint? As time passes, though, her resolve weakens and maybe, just maybe, she can take the risk.

# ABOUT THE AUTHOR

After retiring from her day job of nearly 33 years, Marsha DeFilippo has embarked on a new career of writing books. She is also a lifelong avid crafter and has yet to try a craft she doesn't like. She spends her winters in Arizona and the remainder of the year in Maine.

Visit her site
https://www.marshadefilippo.com

To get the latest information on new releases, excerpts and more, be sure to sign up for Marsha's newsletter.
https://marshadefilippo.com/newsletter

facebook.com/MarshaDeFilippo
twitter.com/marshadefilippo
instagram.com/marshadefilippo

www.ingramcontent.com/pod-product-compliance
Lightning Source LLC
Chambersburg PA
CBHW030624190726

48286CB00008B/2390